A collection of short stories in the Rise of Dragons universe

Magical Liaison Office

G Clatworthy

ISBN: 978-1-915516-37-4

Cover art by Sanjay Charlon (Beehive Illustrations)

Foreword

This is a collection of short stories mainly featuring Agent Jones from the Rise of Dragons universe. Some of these have previously been published in anthologies and some haven't been published before. I have put these in chronological order for ease of reading and I hope you enjoy reading more about Agent Jones.

A special thank you to my husband who reads all of my short stories. You are awesome and I couldn't do this without you!

If you want to support Gemma, you can find her on www.patreon.com/G_Clatworthy for exclusive first reads of new stories. You can also join her newsletter at www.gemmaclatworthy.com for a free prequel to the Rise of Dragons series – and learn a little more about one of Aloora's exes – and follow Gemma on

www.instagram.com/gemmaclatworthy,

www.facebook.com/gemmaclatworthy or join the reader's group on Facebook: Gemma's book wyrms.

The Mirror Crack'd

When someone disappears in a stately home, Agent Jones is called to investigate, but she hadn't bargained on travelling to another realm to solve the case.

This is a never before published story inspired by the title a poem *The Lady of Shalott* by Alfred Tennyson and I later found out it was also the title of an Agatha Christie Miss Marple novel. As she'd one of the authors who inspired me growing up, it felt like it was meant to be.

I pulled up in front of the stately home. Popular tourist destination. Still inhabited by some blue-blooded family. And now host to a crime scene. My standard issue grey Volvo looked out of place in front of something which should have played host to sleek expensive cars. I huffed a sigh of frustration at being called out to this place. It had been a nightmare drive along congested motorways and Maxi, my partner, had been chattering non-stop since we left London. I got out of the car, slammed the door and strode across the gravelled drive. I heard footsteps pounding behind me as Maxi caught up.

"It's amazing to see this place in person! I mean, you get some idea from the guidebooks but nothing compares to the atmosphere of being here, yah? It reminds me of my friend Tarquin's place in the country."

I didn't bother to reply. Mentioning his rich public school boy friends was par for the course. Instead I mounted the stone steps and shook hands with the detective with the crumpled suit waiting for us. His grip was firm and he tried to squeeze hard and show dominance. I suppressed a smile and squeezed back. With my supernatural strength, there was no contest. The look of shock on his face as he felt his bones start to grind together was enough to take the edge off my bad mood. I held on for a second longer then released the handshake. He flexed his hand and I could sense him struggling between annoyed and impressed.

"Jones is it? Glad you're here. You can clear this up no problem I'm sure."

A challenge issued. I returned his gaze coolly, "We'll see what we can do. Why don't you fill me in on what you've got so far?"

"Didn't you read the report? A man's gone missing."

"And you called us because…"

"He disappeared. Into thin air." The detective spoke slowly like I was an idiot. "Could be magic. Thought it was best to get your lot involved just in case."

I arched an eyebrow. So the police had no leads and were bringing the Magical Liaison Office, the organisation I worked for, in so it looked like they were exploring all angles. Typical.

"I want to hear from the witness."

With a nod, he led us to a large room on the ground floor. I stepped through the gilded door and surveyed the scene. It was everything a large room in a country house should be. Oriental rug? Tick. Huge stone fireplace with a carved crest in it? Tick. Massive antique mirror hanging above the fireplace? Tick. Old oil paintings? Tick. It could have been a set for any TV historical drama.

While the detective sent an officer to get the housekeeper - Mrs Troggle - I closed my eyes and inhaled through my nose. Being a lynx shifter, my senses were better than the average humans. Under the pong of tobacco fumes, I got a strong male scent. I guessed that was Lynchworth – the missing man. There was a female too who had been here recently, perhaps the housekeeper. I opened my eyes and followed Lynchworth's most recent scent to the rug in front of the fire. It vanished. I frowned. That was unusual. I looked up and met my own amber eyes in the antique mirror hung over the fire. A hum of magic prickled my senses. I traced the large crack across the surface with my eyes. My first impression was that it was ominous. Stupid word. It was a mirror; that was all. But maybe there was something magical here after all.

The lady who entered wasn't what I expected a housekeeper to be. Especially one with a salt of the earth name like Troggle. She was almost as tall as me, with hair pulled back into a neat bun. She wore a smart black dress and a look of worry in her blue eyes. I could smell the concern coming off her in waves, mixing with her Chanel perfume and the lemony tang of cleaning products. No guilt though. Looked like she hadn't killed him, and I would have been able to scent blood if he had been murdered violently on the premises.

"Good afternoon Ms Troggle, I'm Agent Jones. I'd like to hear in your own words what happened when Mr Lynchworth disappeared."

"It's like I told the police. I was bringing in his tea and I'd arranged the chocolate biscuits he likes on a plate. Anyway I walked in here and he's standing by the fire frowning at the mirror, and he turns and smiles at me and asks me to put the tray on the table. I turned to go and saw him pick up one of those candlesticks. I heard a loud crack and then when I turned back…he was gone. Just like that."

I looked at the lone silver candlestick on the fireplace. Its partner was gone. "And you reported him missing?"

"Well first I called for him you know. Then I looked round the house; there are a few discreet secret passages but none from this room. I tried to get the police involved but they wouldn't have it. They said I had to wait twenty four hours! He could be dead in a ditch by then I said so I called round everywhere he usually went: the local pub, the club in London, his aunt's. No one had seen him so I waited and now they're finally here and poor Mr Lynchworth is gone." She shot a reproachful look at the detective and her bottom lip wobbled. I didn't want to deal with tears.

"Alright. Did he ever say anything about the mirror to you? Or did you see him using it at all?"

She gave me a sharp look, "Well, now that you mention it, I've always thought it was a bit odd."

"Odd how?"

"Well sometimes when I was in here, it seemed like it didn't reflect the room…but then whenever I looked closer it was always normal. And sometimes I'd catch Mr Lynchworth staring at it…you will find him won't you?"

"We'll do our best. Detective, why don't you see Ms Troggle out and make her a cup of tea? Take the officer with you."

The detective wasn't happy I'd effectively dismissed him from his own crime scene but I didn't want any distractions.

"What do you think?" I asked Maxi when I was sure they were out of earshot.

"Secret passages! Better than I expected!"

"Not what I meant."

"Sorry, yah, well could be magic. There are a number of spells that could cause someone to vanish or travel instantaneously."

"Artefacts?" I interrupted before he could launch into a discourse on different types of vanishing spells.

His eyes snapped to mine, "You found something?"

I jerked my head to the mirror. He approached it eagerly and examined it before running his hands through his hair, causing his whitish blonde hair to stand up in a mad professor style that contrasted with his young round face.

"Could be, I'll have to get the equipment out."

He raced back to the car to grab a magic detector of his own design. He pointed the sensor at the mirror while he watched the small screen for readings. "I don't know how you do it! This thing is giving off a strong aura. Can't make out what type of magic it is though."

I was glad he didn't push on how I could sense magic. He didn't know I was a shifter and I wanted to keep it that way. I had some extra abilities that came in handy but I was cautious about who knew; there were still a lot of prejudiced people out there. My magic dampening bracelet stopped my own magical signature from showing on any of our sensors so I was confident he wouldn't find out unless I told him or had to shift in front of him.

I stepped behind him and studied the mirror more closely. It had an extravagant frame, all gold swirls in a baroque style but the mirror itself was spotted with age. I felt the metallic creepy feeling of being too near silver. It was a genuine antique then, not one of these newer aluminium backed mirrors. A large crack ran across the width of it about a third of the way up. The pulse of magic felt stronger there. "Point the sensor here."

Maxi inhaled with a whistle, "The mirror crack'd from side to side! Yah, that's a strong magical field, almost extra dimensional."

"What?"

"Tennyson, you know, The Lady of Shallot – the mirror crack'd from side to side…"

"I don't want to know about the poem! What did you say about dimensions?"

"Oh, the power here, it's almost the same as a portal."

"Schiztz," I swore softly to myself in Dwarfish, the best language for cursing. This was worse than I thought. I called my superior.

He answered on the fourth ring, "What is it Jones?"

"Suspected portal."

"Destination?"

"Unknown."

"What are you proposing?"

"I need access to the Office's portal tech."

"They are developmental only, I can't authorise that. It's too great a risk." Just before I was about to start swearing down the phone, he continued, "You'll have to use your initiative on this one Jones."

"Understood," I hung up. I understood his code. He wouldn't authorise anything but if I could get my hands on the developmental tech another way… "Maxi, who do you know in the research labs?"

A couple of phone calls later and we were still waiting. The detective came back in the room.

"Well?"

"Well what?"

"Any updates?"

"Yes, stay out of this room."

"Now look here, this is my crime scene! Tell me what is going on!"

I pinched the bridge of my nose in frustration before allowing myself to vent a little, "We are here because you suspected magic, which my colleague has just confirmed. That means this is now my jurisdiction and I am ordering you out for your own safety." I watched him swallow. He hadn't really expected anything magical. That made two of us.

"What sort of magic?"

"That's classified. Now get out of *my* crime scene!"

"This is going in my report!"

"Ditto!"

He stormed off. I shrugged. Better he was out of it if there was a portal involved. Who knew where it would lead us?

There was a blinding flash of light and a pearly disk appeared by the sash windows. I turned, my crossbow in my hands instantly. I sighted down it, ready to shoot.

The detective ran back in, his gun out, "What the…?"

I ignored him, focusing on the shimmering disk in front of us. Maxi had his own standard issue crossbow out too and was crouched behind an antique chair, also aiming at the portal.

A figure stepped through. The light from the portal illuminated it from the back so all we could see was the silhouette. The figure was carrying a large box. The portal winked out and we were left looking at a young woman in a lab coat.

"What a welcoming committee!" she quipped.

I put my crossbow back into the holster on my thigh and stepped forward. Maxi pushed past me and took the box from her, "Thanks for coming Bea! Really appreciate it!"

"Is that it?" I nodded at the largish silver box and cut through any chit chat.

She nodded, "Top of the line, fresh from the research department."

"Is it safe?"

There was a slight pause, "Odds are we'll get back in one piece." I didn't like that wording.

"Right, you can head back. This is field work and I don't want you getting hurt."

She shook her head and a steely glint appeared in her eyes, "I don't think so. You need me to operate the machine."

"You can show Maxi how to work it."

She shook her head again, "The dimension fields are sensitive and a language all of their own. I can't teach that in a day."

"We don't have a day! We've got to start moving," Lynchworth had already been stuck in another dimension for over twenty four hours. If he was still alive, we needed to find him and get him back here fast. Big if.

"Another dimension?" the detective's eyes boggled.

I turned to him, using him as a target for my anger at losing control of this situation, "Do you want to join us too?!"

"No, no, I'll just stay here and make sure the scene is secure."

"You do that," I turned back to Bea. Looked like I didn't have a choice, "Right, you can come but you do exactly what I say. And your only job is to stay out of the way and operate that contraption. Understood?"

She nodded. The glint in her eyes turned to excitement. Great. A complete rookie coming on a trip to another dimension. I gestured to the mirror, "Can you figure out where that leads? Don't touch it!"

Bea nodded and approached the mirror again with Maxi, "Looks like a powerful scrying mirror… largest energy field I've encountered. The crack must have destabilised it and created a portal…" They conferred and looked at readings from his magic sensor before Bea made some tweaks to her own machine. I caught phrases like "reverse polarity" and "dimension vortex". I tapped my foot impatiently while they did their work. After fifteen minutes, Bea announced she had configured the portal to the same frequency as the mirror and could get us back to the room.

"Right, let's go," I announced. Bea made to step forward to the mirror, I placed my hand on her shoulder and shook my head, "Age before beauty." I took out my crossbow and reached my hand forward to touch the crack in the mirror.

~

Going through the portal felt like falling sideways combined with being sucked through a vacuum cleaner coupled with the searing heat of silver touching my skin. My vision swam with strange fractal rainbows. I stumbled to one side before shaking my head and regaining my balance. I shook my burnt hand. Damn silver mirrors. Maxi followed, almost falling to the ground as he exited the circular disk. Bea brought up the rear, she seemed more comfortable travelling through the dimensions. I blinked as I took in the circular room. A wooden chair was set up to look at a large mirror, almost exactly the same as the one back in the stately home. I moved my foot over a scuff mark on the flagstone floor. There had been a struggle here. A familiar candlestick lay on the ground. A small arrow-slit window shone a beam of light onto a tapestry set up next to the chair. I moved closer. The intricate embroidery showed a scene I recognised with a jolt. It was the room we'd just come from with a detailed portrait of Lynchworth staring at the viewer. This was creepy. I glanced out of the window. From the cloying feeling at the back of my throat and the strange colours I glimpsed through the slit, we were in one of the fae realms.

I motioned to the others to follow me through the heavy wooden door. It creaked loudly. So much for our visit being a surprise. The door opened onto descending spiral steps. We were in a tower. Great. I kept my crossbow out and followed the steps down.

"This reminds me of that trip to the chateau in Southern France, hey Bea?!"

I hissed at Maxi to be quiet. After two full turns there was another door. I sniffed, trying to lock onto Lynchworth's scent. The tobacco continued down the stairs. I signalled to the humans to follow me when the door opened smoothly. A green-skinned goblin stared at us with boggling eyes. He cried out and turned to flee. I grabbed him and hit him on the head with the handle of my crossbow but it was too late. I could hear more feet stomping our way. Great. I pushed the door and ran into the room. It was a corridor lined with picture windows on one side and large crystal mirrors on the other. The whirling colours of the fae sky reflected onto the floor. It would have been a pleasant effect if it wasn't so creepy. Ten more of the small creatures were moving towards us. They wielded long spears and a couple had swords. An arrow hit the floor by my feet. They had archers too. Great.

I leapt behind a chair pushed against a mirror and loosed off a crossbow bolt. I heard the satisfying thud of the bolt hitting home as one of the archers collapsed. Maxi and Bea cowered behind a large chest. He had his own crossbow out and took down one of the goblins. I reloaded and took aim. My bolt hit one of the archers in the shoulder. He dropped his bow and fell to the ground. I watched from between the legs of the chair as the goblin next to him dived to the floor as well and then lay perfectly still, his eyes closed. He didn't want to be in this fight. Now the archers were dealt with, I holstered my crossbow, picked up the chair with one hand and used it as a battering ram to force my way into the fray. I grabbed a spear from a goblin as I went and wielded it with my free hand. The creatures pressed in on me. I watched as one of Maxi's bolts took out another goblin. The chair was slowing me down. I threw it at a goblin with a sword and a helmet and hit another with the butt of my spear. A cry alerted me to a goblin behind me and I stabbed backwards, thrusting the spear into its stomach. I dropped the spear and picked up a fallen sword. There were four goblins left, looking nervous as they huddled together. They backed away to the far side of the room, knees shaking. It didn't seem right to kill them.

"Where's the human?" I asked.

They looked at each other anxiously. I moved my sword in a threatening way. One of them pointed to the door we had come from. I grunted and went back to the stairwell. Maxi and Bea followed with nervous glances back at the room.

"What if they get reinforcements?"

"I'm not planning to be here that long." I followed the strong smell of tobacco down and down. There was an open door. It led to a dark passageway, devoid of light and windows. I stepped in. My vision adjusted quickly to the dark, plus I had a couple of supernatural senses I could rely on, but by twenty paces in, the two humans were struggling. I rummaged inside my mock crocodile skin handbag. It took a while as the bag was enchanted so it could hold practically anything in the small space, which meant I had to feel through a lot of things before I found what I was looking for. I pulled out a torch and handed it to Maxi. He pressed the switch and lit up our path.

After a while, Maxi asked, "How do you know he went this way?"

A piece of fabric caught my eye, snagged on a nail that stuck out from the wall. I bent forward to retrieve it and twirled it in my fingers. I handed it to Maxi.

"Somehow I don't think they have jeans in the fae realm." I kept going.

The corridor stopped abruptly as the floor came to an end. There was a drop and in the chasm was a series of walls. They reflected Maxi's torchlight as he came up behind me. My brain caught up with my eyes. The walls were made from mirrors.

"You'll never find him you know," a figure in white spoke from across the chasm, "I've trapped him here so I can be free." The figure let out a little giggle and lights sprang from her fingers. The mirrors bounced the beams across the maze walls. My eyes adjusted to the new light. The figure was a woman in a long white dress with bronze hair cascading down her shoulders. Her blue eyes had a crazed look to them.

"Who are you?"

"Who am I? Do you know, I have quite forgotten my name! I have been trapped here so long, but now I will be free! No more mirrors to see the worlds, I will make my own way."

"And Lynchworth?"

"A pity I suppose but he was so easy to talk to, to convince of my plight…he broke the mirror and now he will replace me. I will be free!" With another hysterical giggle, she ran off. Great.

"Lynchworth?" I called. There was a muffled reply then a banging noise as he hit the glass. "Keep making noise, we'll get you out." Guess we were going into a mirror maze. I fished in my bag and retrieved a length of rope. I looped one end around my waist and told Maxi and Bea to climb down. With some trepidation, they moved down the rope one by one. After they were safely down, I jumped into the chasm and landed in a crouch on the glass floor. We followed the maze until I walked headfirst into a mirror. I rubbed my forehead and cursed in Dwarfish. Using my hand, I felt my way along until we came to a gap in the mirrors. We turned through and I stopped as strings of sticky silk looped across the mirrored corridor.

The smell of tobacco was strong here. Lynchworth was this way. I pinched the bridge of my nose as I tried to think. There was nothing for it. I told Maxi and Bea to stay put and keep watch. No point getting them in trouble too. I ducked under the web and moved forward. Nothing moved. I carried on and then I was through. The corridor led to a dead end but there, tucked into one corner was Lynchworth. He was wrapped in thick silk and was kicking against the mirrored wall. Carefully, I used the sword's blade to cut the web surrounding him. Lynchworth's face goggled at me. It was a blueish colour but he was alive. He tried to speak but a strange choking sound came out. I couldn't make out any words. I whispered that we were here to help and pulled him to his feet. He wobbled, dangerously close to falling over.

"What's there? Have you found something?" Maxi's voice sounded loud over the quiet in this maze.

I hissed at him to shut up before hoisting Lynchworth over my shoulder in a fire fighter's lift. I edged back the way I'd come. That's when I noticed the threads vibrating. I moved faster. Maxi and Bea were both staring at a spot above my head. Their faces were mirror images of horror. Great. I'd seen enough movies to know not to turn around. Instead I used my sword to cut through the threads like a machete and hurried on. I dumped Lynchworth at their feet as soon as I was free of the webs, drew my crossbow and finally turned around. Straight into the hideous face of a tarfangtula. A massive spider like creature with ten legs and the same number of bulbous purple eyes. I took in the pedipalps thicker than my forearm and pointed teeth as it bore down on me. I aimed my crossbow straight into its drooling maw and fired. It reared up in pain, exposing its belly. Maxi's torch shone onto the blue hairs that covered its stomach. I shot again. Another bolt hit alongside mine as Maxi joined in. Yellow slime oozed from the wound.

"Run!" I yelled, hefting Lynchworth back onto my shoulder. With the added weight I was barely faster than the humans and I made sure they stayed in front of me as we fled. My high heels made purchase on the glass floor difficult. I slipped as we rounded a corner. A shriek from behind told me that the creature was pursuing us. There was no contest. Ten legs to our two each. It caught up.

"Open the portal!"

Bea stared at me, looked up at the giant spider reflected in the mirrors, then snapped out of whatever daze she was in. She ducked into another turning in the maze and pushed a button. A swirling opalescent disk appeared. I pushed Lynchworth at Maxi and Bea, "Get him through!"

They took an arm each and dragged him through the portal. Maxi looked back as he went through and I shouted that I'd be there soon. Free of the worry of protecting others and being discovered as a shifter, I faced the tarfangtula and changed. As a large lynx, I was more agile than in my human form. We eyed each other for a moment. It lunged. I dodged to the side, jumped and rebounded off the wall to land on its back. I dug my claws in, feeling them cut into its thick hide. It shrieked with pain and reared up again. I used its own momentum to slide down its back and take it off balance. Just before it hit the ground, I jumped. It landed on its back, legs flailing wildly. I pounced onto its underside and raked its belly. It screamed again but its legs were slowing. I leapt off and winced as the yellow goop from its innards burnt my skin. Poison. Great.

I headed to the portal and prepared to shift back to my human form when another sound made my ears prick. Loud, regular taps. The maze began to shake. I turned back to see a large creature round the corner. It was reflected over and over in the mirrored walls. I blinked twice as I tried to take in the gigantic killer bird in front of me. It clawed the tarfangtula's body with razor talons two feet long and stuck its sharp beak into the carcass. I heard a clacking as it began to rip legs from the body and devour them. I backed away towards the portal. Maybe it hadn't seen me. The movement drew its beady black eyes. It let out a roar that sounded like a crow crossed with an elephant. Great. It stepped over the carcass and flexed its huge feathered wings. Beak open, it snaked its head towards me.

I leapt towards it and landed on its hooked beak. It cawed again and shook its head from side to side as it tried to get me off. I jumped again and I was on top of its crest. The greasy purple feathers made it difficult to get purchase. I flexed my claws desperately as I slipped to the side. I managed to get purchase and the giant bird cawed again and lowered its head, scraping me against a wall. I let go to avoid being crushed and scrabbled at the top of the wall. I managed to get up and I ran along the narrow walls of the maze.

"It's losing power!" I heard Bea's disembodied voice through the dimensions. The portal shimmered and start to shrink. Great. I thought for a second about the mysterious crazy lady then pushed her from my mind as the portal shrank again. I forced myself to move, sprinting towards it. I leapt and shifted into my human form as I ploughed into the portal. Shifting whilst travelling to another dimension was a mistake. I stumbled to the side and threw up as the drawing room swam into view. I heard a scream. The humongous killer bird had tried to follow me. I turned and aimed my crossbow at the portal, still shaking from inter-dimensional travel. Before I could loose off a bolt, the portal winked shut, severing the monster in two. I watched as its head twitched before falling lifeless on the oriental rug.

~

The clean-up crew arrived quickly. Gwen entered the room and surveyed the scene, her dove grey wings beat softly and she gave an impressed whistle as she took in the severed head.

"Well, well, Jones, I don't think I've ever had to clean up a terror bird before."

"Just keeping you on your toes."

"This it?"

"He needs a medic. Tarfangtula poison," I pointed my thumb at the prone Lynchworth we had laid on a red and gold antique sofa, "And the mirror."

The harpy nodded and barked orders at her team. They moved with efficiency. A small fae medic dealt with the human whilst another team member incinerated the decapitated head without singeing the rug.

"Be careful!" I couldn't help shouting as two team members in protective haz mat suits moved towards the mirror. They nodded at me and lifted it by the frame. As soon as it was off the wall, they staggered under its weight. I met Gwen's gaze and we both sighed before taking over carrying it by the decorative frame. Sometimes there was no substitute for supernatural strength. We manoeuvred it out of the stately home and into the clean-up team's grey van parked at an angle on the drive.

"You're not going to destroy it?" I asked.

Gwen shook her head, "Orders are to take it in. The Office is very interested in all forms of portal magic at the moment." She shrugged and then covered the mirror with a large linen cloth. The hum of magic disappeared instantly. Containment ward woven into the cloth. At least I knew they'd be safe getting back to the London branch.

"Well looks like you've saved the day again, Jones."

It was my turn to shrug, "All in a day's work."

Summer Solstice in Swindon

When you work for the Magical Liaison Office, the Summer Solstice can be a giant party, or you can get dragged in to dealing with magic roundabouts and monsters.

This story was first published in the Summer Solstice Shenanigans anthology in 2021 and was the first story I earned something from, so it has a special place in my heart.

Chapter One

Today was not a good day. It hadn't been ever since I had received the call from my superior. Instead of supervising the biggest Summer Solstice event in the UK at Stonehenge, enjoying the party atmosphere, I was going to Swindon. The only thing I knew about the town was that it had once been voted one of the most miserable places to live in the UK. Great.

I drove my standard issue grey Volvo through the police roadblocks and parked in an empty discount supermarket carpark. I got out of the car and slammed the door, not attempting to hide my annoyance. My partner, Maxi, got out the other side, fiddling with the straps on his backpack as he grabbed the radar equipment he'd invented.

A small gnome with grey hair and a bulbous nose waved at us before walking over. Sweat caused his white formal shirt to cling to him in the afternoon sun. "Agent Jones?"

I nodded and he breathed an audible sigh of relief. As a shifter, my senses are heightened. I could smell the anxiety pouring off him.

"Thank goodness you came, I'm in way over my head. The ground started rumbling this morning. I came as soon as I could of course, but, I mean, I run the local museum of magic, it's not like I'm used to this sort of thing."

This sort of thing. Meaning any magical disturbance that could threaten the balance between humans and magical beings. Exactly the sort of thing the Magical Liaison Office, my employers, dealt with.

I rubbed my eyes and pinched the bridge of my nose, "The ground isn't rumbling now." I pointed out.

The gnome's eyes widened and he looked around. No help there.

"Alright Maxi, let's scan the area."

Maxi pulled out his equipment in preparation. He ran his hands through his hair, causing it to stick up further in a mad professor style that sat oddly with his youthful face.

I made my own survey of the so called magic roundabout, striding through the heat haze rising from the tarmac. It looked crazy to me. Five small roundabouts surrounded one larger one and judging from the traffic markings, every car could go in any direction. I was glad I hadn't had to learn to drive here.

I sniffed cautiously. I hated people knowing I was a shifter, but the amplified senses came in handy. Oil, metal and exhaust fumes came up from the tarmac, but there was something else too. I bent down to kneel in the centre of one of the white mini roundabouts. Elf.

A dart of movement in the corner of my eye made me turn my head. A cloaked figure stepped from the shadows of a nearby house and raised its arms.

"Stop right there!" I yelled. The figure turned and sprinted away, obviously. I stood up, ready to give chase, then heard a sucking noise as a portal opened behind me. I turned and looked straight into the ten shining purple eyes of a giant tarfangtula. A horse-sized spider creature straight from the fae realm. I knew this was going to be a bad day!

The monster let out a shriek, showing sharp teeth behind its protruding pedipalps and lunged at me. I jumped to the side, narrowly avoiding its bite and drew my weapon from the holster strapped to my waistband.

I flicked off the safety and loosed off a shot from the handheld crossbow, glad I kept it loaded. The silver tipped bolt was enchanted with fire and it lit up on contact with the giant spider's head.

I took the chance to reload quickly and glanced at the closing portal. At least nothing else was coming through. I shouted at the uniformed officers to "Stay back!" They wouldn't be much use with batons and tasers anyway and I didn't want any casualties.

I circled around the spider as the creature howled both in pain and anger. It shook its ugly head and rushed at me again. It was too fast, its ten long legs outpacing my two and it closed its jaws on my arm, tearing through my linen suit.

I shot the crossbow from point blank range, turning my face as the bolt ignited on contact. The tarfangtula let go and backed up a few steps, the claws on the ends of its legs thudding on the tarmac.

Another bolt hit its abdomen and I glanced over at Maxi, still in the carpark and shaking as he tried to reload his own crossbow. The creature turned to glare at this new threat and started to run towards him.

"Dzrak." I swore to myself in dwarfish, the best language for swearing among all species. I hated shifting in public but Maxi was only human and likely to get killed. I began to run towards it, my heels clicking on the road's surface. Shifting into my large lynx form, I jumped onto the giant spider's back. My claws scrabbled on its hard body before finding purchase, its dark blue hairs bristling as it felt me land. It reared up, trying to shake me off, but I bit down hard, my jaws piercing the shell over its abdomen.

Yellow goo from its innards filled my mouth, burning my lips and spilling out across its back. My paws started to tingle too. Of course it was poisonous. I jumped off before it started to do some real damage, I didn't have time to waste healing today.

The creature was in trouble. Maxi had loosed off a couple more bolts into its head. Its legs curled and it seemed to fall back into itself. I growled as it fell twitching to the floor. I tilted my head, listening for a heartbeat. Nothing. Its yellow blood oozed out over the road, hissing slightly.

I shifted back and walked slowly towards my partner. He was both staring and trying to play it cool.

"You're a shifter!"

I nodded, wishing I had thought to have the conversation with him earlier. It comes as a shock when your work buddy turns out to be a supernatural being, but he was holding up well.

"The sensors didn't pick you up!" He gestured to the radar he'd been setting up before the portal had opened.

I sighed and shook my wrist so the golden bracelet I wore showed clearly, noting the red burns from the tarfangtula's blood on my tanned skin. "This hides my magical signature, comes in handy for the day job."

"And your clothes…"

I turned my gaze up to a glare, "You did do the species training course, right?" He nodded, wide eyed at my tone, "Then you know that clothes and whatever we're carrying form part of the transformation, it's part of the shifter magic."

He went back to fiddling with the radar, "All ready boss." Good, we were done talking about my abilities. I grimaced at the red burns on my skin. The pain was intensifying as the poison worked its way into my human skin.

"Give me a minute." I strode back to the car and grabbed a small green bottle from the glove box. Madam Mim's *Cure All,* perfect for speeding up my natural healing and stopping the tingling electric feeling still going on in my mouth. I took a swig and carefully poured some on the burns and the bite mark on my arm, the red sores calming almost instantly.

Dosed up, I marched back, picked up one of the radar machines and started slowly walking over the magic roundabout. Maxi took the other side.

~

It didn't take long to finish the survey and I tapped my foot impatiently as Maxi loaded the data into a laptop and brought up the combined visual. He had modified the radar equipment to show magical energies as well as mundane features. I inhaled sharply.

Underneath each of the mini roundabouts was a clear rune, outlined in wizard magic that glowed purple on the monitor. The runes were connected with glowing leylines across the five roundabouts to form a pentagram. There was more magic in the centre but we couldn't get a clear reading. The mundane part of the radar picked up a large cavern deep underground. I hadn't encountered a magical seal before but this one was big and judging by the size of the cavern, it needed to be. I pinched the bridge of my nose, what had we gotten into?

Before I could say anything, Maxi pointed at the screen, "Look! It's failing!" I leaned closer. One of the runes was glowing less brightly than the rest and the lines connecting it to the rest of the pentagram were weaker too. Great.

I considered calling it in and getting some back-up, but the Office would be stretched with all the Solstice celebrations going on across the country and I didn't even know what we were dealing with. Apparently neither did my superiors or they wouldn't have sent a two person team out to deal with this level of magical incident. I rubbed the back of my neck in frustration and decided to take it out on the gnome that had called it in.

"Right," I called over to the small magical being who had been hovering, unsure if he should leave, but not wanting to go without my permission. "You run the local museum of magic right? This is a magical seal. You called us. What do you know about it?"

The gnome blinked and his shirt was now soaked with sweat. He definitely knew something. "Well, I, er, you see, it's been in place for centuries, I just never thought…" he broke off, on the point of tears. Sniffing, he continued, "I mean, it should be fine for now, everyone knows the best time to breach realms is when the fabric of realities lessens at sunrise and sunset on the days of the Solstice."

I sighed and decided to play nice, "Why don't we go to the museum and you can show us what you know there? Can you ward this place for us to help the police out in case someone comes back before sunset?"

The small gnome nodded, I had guessed right, he was a magic user. He raised his arms outwards, grey magic flowed from him as he channelled his power to form a pentagon shaped dome around the roundabout. I caught some of the police officers looking our way suspiciously. Being human, they couldn't see the magic, but giant killer spiders and shifters were harder to explain.

Maxi retrieved our crossbow bolts from the corpse; the Office was keen on reusing magical weaponry. Then he and the gnome got into the car while I spoke to the officer in charge. "I'm sending in a clean-up crew for that," I pointed over my shoulder with my thumb, "we'll be back soon, the gnome has information. Call me if anything suspicious happens." I handed him a card from one of my pockets.

"Like what?"

I gave the officer a look. "Well, if you see any more hooded figures, massive arachnids, or the ground starts shaking. You know, stuff like that."

He was blinking at me but managed to reply, "So end of the world stuff, got it."

I snorted a laugh despite myself, maybe I could get to like this officer. I nodded and turned, lifting my phone to my ear to call in the tarfangtula. Normally I'd stay to supervise the clean-up but the museum wasn't far and I planned to be back before they'd finished.

Chapter Two

The gnome's hands shook as he unlocked the museum on the edge of town. I could see why it had been voted one of the unhappiest places to live in the UK. Nondescript grey buildings loomed nearby and derelict shops lined the part of the High Street I could see. Not exactly social media snap-worthy.

The museum was in a squat concrete building with a carved wooden door and a small brass plaque proclaiming itself as a museum of magic, run by Nerdok Neebly. I guessed it didn't get many visitors.

Once inside, the gnome's posture straightened and he seemed to feel more at ease. The coolness of the building was welcome as the heat of the afternoon was still intense outside and I breathed more easily too.

We padded over rich carpets and past small glass cases holding magical artefacts, as the gnome led us to his office.

He took a seat behind a large mahogany leather-topped desk and gestured for us to sit on the two uncomfortable-looking chairs opposite. I sat and leaned forward, placing my hands on my knees.

"Right, Mr, uh, Neebly, tell us everything. Fast."

Neebly held his hands up in a pacifying gesture, "Look, first off, it's not like I was expecting this at all. I wanted a cushy job inside, not many people, where I could study." He gestured at the books lining his office, "But, my predecessor did mention the seal and, technically, I'm a guardian." He looked miserable, "It comes with the role, but the seal has been quiet for centuries. No one even knows it's there anymore. I never thought I'd have to…I mean, I'm not equipped for…"

I reached over and put my hand on the desk with a slap, "In my experience Neebly, no one is equipped for things like this. Now, I want to help, I really do, but I need to know what is under that seal and anything you know about who might be trying to unlock it."

He took a deep breath and got up, pulling back a false bookshelf to reveal an old-looking safe. He turned the dial several times and it unlocked with an anti-climactic clunk. He pulled out a book bound in red leather and a sheaf of newspaper clippings.

"The seal was created by Merlin himself, when the last dragons roamed the earth. This was a small dwelling then, out of the way and near places of power, like Stonehenge and Avebury, that bolstered the magic. Every fifty years or so, one of the Wizard's Council checks the runes and adds power. The next visit is due next year."

"So this is the weakest point in the cycle, what!" I gave Maxi a look. He was enthusiastic about everything and sometimes sounded like a public school boy.

Neebly didn't seem to have noticed, "Exactly right. As I said, the solstices are the time when the fabric between realities is thinnest and so the perfect time for reinforcing the seal…or attempting to destroy it."

Neebly scattered the newspaper clippings onto the desk, some were yellowed with age and one was from last week.

"Over time, there have been attempts to break the seal, but the last one was in the seventies and was thwarted by the guardian at the time, a wizard called Halberd." I nodded, I'd heard of him, but was surprised he'd accepted a post to curate this museum.

"That's when it was decided to build the magic roundabout to more clearly hide the runes." He caught our looks of surprise, "Oh yes, this goes all the way to the top: the town planning committee." I blinked and he carried on, "The cars that drive over it actually reinforce it, if they go clockwise."

I thought back to the roundabout, "But it looks like cars can go round that anti-clockwise too…"

Neebly shifted uncomfortably, "Well, yes, the committee made a bit of an oversight there and unfortunately those going anticlockwise can weaken the seal. But we never really thought it was a problem. After all, the effect is counteracted by other cars and the seal is strengthened regularly."

I raised an eyebrow but refrained from saying anything.

"One of the guardian's roles is to keep an eye on the seal and note any strange goings on. Last week there were anti-social behaviour reports in the local paper of hooded figures in midsummer. A cult." He tapped the most recent article and I scanned it. Strange bangs had been heard and glowing lights had been seen near figures wearing hooded clothing. The paper was blaming gothic teenagers, but I supposed it could have been magical.

"What exactly are they trying to unseal Neebly?" I fixed my amber eyes on the squirming gnome.

He opened the ancient book and pushed it across to me. Maxi leaned in close to read over my shoulder.

The first thing I saw was the picture. The artist had clearly gone all out for horror by medieval standards and it was gruesome. A gargantuan crimson beast stood on hoofed feet, bat-like wings spread above it as it tore a human in half. Its face was buried in its victim's torso, large teeth protruding through the flesh. I pulled my eyes to the text. Latin. Typical. I was about to make a comment to Neebly when Maxi spoke up.

"A demon! An actual demon!"

"You read Latin?"

He shrugged, "Didn't you learn at school?!"

I made a mental note to ask which school he had gone to. "I'm a little rusty. Give me the gist of it."

His mouth moved as he translated, then he looked at me, his pale blue eyes wide, "It's called an Avesuspapercabra!"

"Abracadabra?" I didn't even attempt to get the name right.

Maxi rolled his eyes and corrected me, adding "It's nasty! It can fly, and breathe fire! But that's not the worst part! It guards the entrance to a demon realm that has been closed off for over a millennium!"

"You're telling me that the gates of hell are underneath a roundabout in Swindon?!"

"In a nutshell, yes!"

Great. No wonder this town had a bad reputation. I dreaded to think what was underneath the worst town in the UK.

"Right, how do we fix the seal?" I was no nonsense when it came to this sort of thing. In my experience, the quicker we got to the solution the better.

"Erm, well a wizard could strengthen the seal, but the Council is incommunicado because of the Solstice." Neebly chimed in. I glared at him, unfairly blaming him for being unable to contact the Wizarding High Council.

"OK, try to get a wizard here before sunrise. Got it. Plan B?"

"As guardian, I do have an…artefact…for emergencies."

I stared at him, my eyes unblinking and I knew my pupils were narrowing as I fought to control my anger and keep my shifter form at bay. This was exactly the sort of thing we needed and he was telling us now!

He got the message and went back to the safe to retrieve the relic. He placed a package bound in oilskin cloth on the desk and unwrapped it reverently to reveal a jewelled dagger. Rubies glinted in its hilt and symbols I didn't recognise covered its blue steel blade. I could feel the magic emanating from it.

"If this is plunged into the demon by a guardian, it will perish."

My expression turned from interest to horror at imagining this gnome facing off with a giant demon from hell. Neebly had turned a greenish colour as he had similar thoughts. Then he grabbed the book and started turning pages frantically.

"I could swear you in as a guardian." I looked around the office pointedly, I had no intention of quitting the Magical Liaison Office to set up as a museum curator. He shook his head and waved a hand dismissively, "The curator position is not obligatory, I'll swear you both in."

I held up my hand, "This sounds important. What exactly does a guardian do?"

Neebly sighed, "It's a sacred role to guard the world from magical threats. Similar to your job really. Each eldritch seal has a guardian watching it…"

"There's more than one!"

"Oh yes, quite a number really. I don't actually know how many, it's not like we have conventions!" Neebly laughed drily at his own joke, "As I said, it's been more of a technicality for me. I suppose it sounded exciting when I was younger but I never really expected this and now…Anyway, I can swear you in and then the dagger will activate for you, as will other guardian objects."

I tried to think of another option but failed and we were running out of time before sunset. I caught Maxi's eye and he gave me a nod.

"Fine." I huffed.

Neebly's eyes lit up and he immediately recited some words in a foreign language. Latin, I guessed. Translucent magic curled in his hands as he recited. Then he reached out and touched us both on our hands. A rune appeared then settled into my skin before disappearing. I didn't feel any different.

"It's done." Neebly sank onto his chair and offered me the dagger.

"Oh no, you're not getting out of this so easily, guardian. You're coming with us."

Chapter Three

I let Maxi take the wheel for the short drive back while I put in a call to my superior about rounding up a wizard from a local Solstice event.

"Let me get this clear Jones. You want me to find a member of the Wizarding High Council with no notice and get them to Swindon before sunset in…" I could hear him checking the chunky rolex he always wore… "ten minutes!"

"Yes well, there's a demon…" I tried to explain the urgency of our situation but he cut me off.

"I've got elves climbing on Stonehenge, dwarves trying to burn effigies in the Welsh hills and the media is crawling over everything. And I just got a call from Gwendoline telling me you weren't even there to meet the clean-up team you requested." I winced, I had hoped to be back before they were done. "I don't have time for this. Just handle it!" He hung up. Great, it looked like we were on our own.

Maxi parked up outside the roadblock. I nodded to the officer in charge, still on duty, and flashed my badge as we strode past. He didn't even move and stayed staring straight ahead.

"The world didn't end while we were away then?" I joked. Nothing. I moved closer and waved my hand in front of his eyes. He didn't even blink. Standing this close to him I noticed the faint aura of magic on him. I turned slowly, my keen eyes taking in other officers, all equally frozen in various guard positions. One was frozen mid step as she walked to her post. This was not good.

I hustled Maxi and Neebly to the low wall surrounding the carpark and crouched low, gesturing for them to copy me.

"Looks like we've got company. Someone's bespelled all the humans at the roadblocks. The Office isn't sending a wizard so we're on our own here."

Neebly swallowed hard. Maxi loaded his crossbow. I did the same and grabbed the dagger.

"The plan is to stop whatever's about to happen before it happens. Got it?" It was a rubbish plan, but it was all I had.

I peeked over the top of the wall. Cloaked figures were apparating onto the magic roundabout. Six in total. Five stood on the smaller white roundabouts and one stood in the centre. The middle figure pushed back his hood revealing a bald head, pointed elven ears and an equally pointed neat goatee. He looked like a clerk in a bank, not who I envisaged as the leader of a cult. I sniffed deeply and recognised his scent from earlier. So he had portal magic and was strong enough to deactivate Neebly's ward. This was going to be bad.

He raised his arms into the air and twisted them, curling magic around them. I sprang over the wall and shouted out.

"This is an unauthorised area for Solstice celebrations and magic use." I made that up, but it sounded official. "I'm going to have to ask you to cease and desist… and leave."

I started to walk towards them, deliberately slowing my pace to appear confident. I stepped over a yellow stain on the road that was all that was left of the tarfangtula. The clean-up team was efficient, I'll give them that. I just wished they had taken a bit longer, I could have used any help I could have got.

The central figure laughed, a strange clipped sound as if he'd read about laughing but never tried it for real, "Aha, very good. I'm impressed you managed to dispatch the tarfangtula without any magical abilities, but we are on a deadline here and you are getting in the way."

He sent a bolt of magic towards me. I dodged left and it hit the wall behind me, charring the stone. He frowned at my unexpected agility. Thank you magic-dampening bracelet, surprise might be the only thing we had going for us.

I pulled out my crossbow. "Last time I'm going to ask. You need to leave. Now."

The elf laughed again and this time his magic connected, hard. It pushed me to the ground and pinned me. I gasped as the pressure built. A crossbow bolt whistled overhead, striking one of the cultists in the shoulder. The pressure eased a little as the elf's attention shifted. Thank you Maxi. More energy swirled through the air as he conjured another spell and sent it soaring towards my partner. Maxi didn't have my supernatural reflexes but he managed to step to one side so the bolt hit his arm rather than his chest. He slumped to the ground in pain.

"Sir, the sun!" One of the hooded figures cried out, as the light began to disappear. Satisfied we weren't going to cause any trouble, the leader turned back to his conjuring.

Neebly stuck his head out from behind the wall and I sensed his magic flowing around me, creating a barrier between me and the elf's magic. I wriggled tentatively. I could move. But I didn't want to blow my one chance at stopping this. I raised my crossbow slowly, trying not to draw attention to my movement. I needn't have worried. The elf had a look of ecstasy on his face as he worked his ritual. The others were watching intensely.

The large runes we had seen on the radars began to shimmer and rise up, the connecting lines between them now visible. Each cultist seemed to glow red as they added their own magic to their leader's energy.

I took aim and loosed a bolt. The energy from whatever ritual they were doing incinerated my bolt as it entered the boundaries of the roundabout.

The elf turned to face me as he felt something disturb the magical field and laughed. "Aha! You are too late. He comes!"

~

I pushed myself up and was running towards them when the ground rumbled and split open, right in the middle of the roundabout. I backed up fast, not wanting to get sucked into a sinkhole and found myself next to Maxi who was slumped against the brick wall.

The elf's magic faltered as he jumped to keep his balance and the others staggered back to make space for the hole opening.

Two enormous arms clawed their way up out of the crater and the creature lifted itself out, landing hard on the road with a roar that made me cover my sensitive ears.

I remembered a bit of trivia Maxi had told me on the drive over: Swindon meant "pig hill". It seemed almost poetic that the demon trapped underneath it partially resembled a swine. Although that was massively understating its menacing appearance.

It stood on the tarmac, stamping huge hooves on the hard ground and shaking out its bat-like wings. Bristling dark red hairs covered its entire body, which became human-like in the torso and arms. Its head was shaped like a boar from hell, complete with sharp tusks pointing out at all angles from its snout. The creature's eyes flamed orange and, above its flat ears, two curled horns swept upwards. It stared around and roared again, lifting its hideous head towards the sky. It almost seemed to glow in the light of the setting sun.

"All right, Abracadabra, let's go!" I muttered, reloading my crossbow and trying to block out the stench of sulphur, pig and goat musk that emanated from the demon and hit my heightened sense of smell so hard I could feel a headache coming on.

"Avesuspapercabra!" Maxi corrected me with a weak smile. I rolled my eyes and darted forwards, loosing off a shot towards its head.

The bolt connected and burst into flames. The monster roared louder this time and fixed its beady orange eyes on me. It pawed the ground with its hooves like a bull, lowered its head and charged. I darted out of its path but it stretched out one massive hand and managed to grab my braided hair. I cried out as it yanked me backwards, cursing my own vanity at keeping my hair long, then I shifted. Short fur is harder to get a hold of than a long plait and I raced off on all fours.

The demon roared again, spitting flames into the air in frustration. It bent its head and began to chase me. I heard a hideous squelching crunching noise as it stepped on one of the cultists who was trying to get out of the way. The others were huddled near the exit for the football stadium, looking on with awe at what they had unleashed. I led the creature towards them, but the head elf put up a magical shield. I saw it just in time and leapt, using it as a springboard to change direction.

The demon crashed through the shield as it turned to follow me. I heard the elf cry out in pain as his shield was destroyed. I gave a growl of satisfaction and kept going. I sensed more magic and risked turning my head to see a portal appearing. I doubled back, circling behind the creature and dived straight for the elf. His attention was on the portal and I connected hard. I tore into him with my claws, making sure he was disabled and trusting his elven healing abilities would prevent him from actually dying.

The other cultists drew back as I snarled. I decided they weren't the priority and turned back to the monster.

It was dragging a hoof on the ground as it faced Maxi, who had managed to shoot off another crossbow bolt. I saw Neebly's white translucent magic forming a shield, but it didn't feel strong compared to the energy pouring off the demon. I bounded around the crater between us and jumped. I landed on the demon's back and clawed my way up its wings, ripping the fragile membrane. It reached over its shoulder but I stayed out of reach as it howled in pain. It staggered back and I let go, jumping to the ground.

One of its flailing hooves connected with my side and I felt at least one rib break. I landed badly, winding myself. I tried to recover but wasn't quick enough. It grabbed me round the middle with one of its clawed hands and squeezed tightly. I yelped in pain as my ribs crunched together. It brought me up to its ugly pig face and roared again. I closed my eyes against the force of its roar, my sensitive ears deafened in this close proximity to it.

It sniffed me and opened its mouth wide, bringing me close to its terrible jaws. I took a breath and then transformed back to my human form, wincing as my broken body shifted. I raised the dagger that had returned now I was defurred and plunged it into its nose up to the hilt. The rune on my hand reappeared, glowing white against my tanned skin. The rubies embedded in the dagger's hilt began to glow and I felt the power from the artefact grow.

The creature howled and dropped me to claw at the dagger sticking from its snout. I shifted again mid fall and landed hard, but upright, on my lynx feet.

Ruby red light began to shine like a beacon from the knife and the demon disintegrated slowly, burning up from its muzzle outwards. Its shrieks hung in the air even after it had disappeared.

Over the ringing in my ears, I heard sucking noises from the other side of the hole and turned in time to see a portal closing. The cultists had all disappeared, taking their stricken leader with them.

I padded over to Maxi, limping as I tried to favour my broken ribs. He was pale and burnt all down one side from the bolt of magic. I shifted again to my human form.

"You did good," I patted his good shoulder, "Neebly, get the *Cure All* from the car."

Neebly was shaking but managed to retrieve the small green bottle. I dripped some into Maxi's mouth and splashed it on his wounds before taking a sip myself. I rubbed a small amount on my side. It took away the immediacy of the pain, but it wouldn't mend my ribs. I trusted my own healing abilities would do that overnight.

The police officers, freed from their frozen states and seeing a humongous hole where a roundabout had been, ran over to help.

"End of the world huh?" the officer in charge goggled at me.

"You have no idea." I muttered.

Epilogue

Three wizards turned up about five minutes later. They had felt the magical energy reverberate through Wiltshire and had decided to investigate. Typical! You want one wizard then three come at once.

They sorted out the residual magic that hung over the roads, healed Maxi fully and then spent all Solstice night recasting the seal. Apparently one can never be too careful with a potential hellgate. I kept my mouth shut when one of them came out with that line after being conveniently absent when we were trying to prevent the seal from breaking and all hell breaking lose.

Maxi was driving us back to London as my ribcage still hurt like hell – pun intended – I had waved away wizarding healing, trusting my own, slower abilities more. My phone rang. I winced as I retrieved it from my pocket and pulled a face as I recognised the caller ID of my superior.

"Jones. What's this I hear about a demon?!" he yelled down the phone. I held it away from my sensitive ears that had just about recovered from the demon's roars. "It's all over social media. We've had to explain it away as a massive gas explosion. Swindon's town planning committee have called me! This couldn't be a bigger mess!"

That was when I lost my cool. "It's not my fault that you sent a two person team to deal with a cult trying to summon a creature from hell. What did you think would happen?! You're lucky we handled that thing and it didn't get loose and open up a portal to the demon realm!"

"Alright, alright. I guess you did the best you could, given the circumstances, but look Jones, the powers that be are not happy with this exposure for our Office. I think it's best you lay low for a while, so I'm transferring you."

I blinked at the phone. A transfer? What the hell?

"You're going to our Cardiff branch until this blows over. I don't want to hear any arguments. See me first thing tomorrow to go through the paperwork."

I took a breath and forced myself to spit out corporate jargon that I knew would unnerve him more than shouting. "I'm glad you're calling me in. I'd like a chance to go through the gross negligence and reckless disregard for two of your agents' lives when you sent us out on this job and refused my request for wizard back-up earlier this evening."

I could hear him thinking over the ramifications to his career before he answered more carefully. "Hmmm, yes, well, perhaps your transfer could be turned into a promotion, they do need someone to head up the Welsh office. See me tomorrow and we'll talk." He hung up.

I gazed out of the car window. From the motorway, I could see bonfires and fireworks lighting up the horizon as the rest of the magical community continued to celebrate the Summer Solstice.

Maxi reached over to pat my shoulder. I'd known today was going to be a bad day.

A Manticore on the Loose

Two strange men arrive at the Magical Liaison Office in Wales, asking about a lost manticore. Can Agent Jones find it before it causes any trouble?

This story was first published in the 2024 Magically Wild anthology where all the writers were given a prompt around creatures escaping for another realm. I enjoyed writing this one as I tied it in with a reference in Equinox Betrayal and Darkest Deception, so now you know how Agent Jones knew the elf who helps the team lure the dragons to the elven reserve of Breconia.

I pinched the bridge of my nose and leaned back in my chair before turning my attention to the two people seated in front of my desk.

"So you've lost a manticore."

One of them fidgeted with a gold bangle, one of two – the other silver, around their wrist. Magic emanated from it, and my hand went to the magic dampening cuff around my arm.

"We have discussed this already, Agent Jones." The smaller one sighed. I frowned. My eyes told me that his lips didn't quite match his speech, and it was giving me a headache.

My nostrils flared. They weren't human, but they weren't a supernatural race I'd encountered before either. Their scent held a whiff of brimstone mixed with something sweet.

"And you can't tell me who you really are," I said.

The large male blanched, but the smaller figure just twitched his lips and shook his head. I tapped my cuff again. Who was I to judge if they wanted to hide their true nature? My cuff was designed to hide my own abilities from those who could sense magic, after all.

"Or why you're keeping a manticore despite them being a protected species."

"We have all the relevant permits."

"I'm sure you do." I sighed. "And you're certain it's somewhere in Wales." It was a stupid thing to say. Even if it was outside my jurisdiction, I'd help hunt it down. Manticores weren't pets, they were dangerous creatures. A class five on the protected species register, ranking them as high, and as vicious, as the man-eating basilisk. Or, as I preferred to call them; dzraking dangerous. They were only permitted in named habitats that had the reserves to make sure they didn't get out.

"We are."

"But you're not going to tell me how you know that." It wasn't a question. These two had shown up at the Magical Liaison Office with an urgent request but no real information other than there was a manticore running around Wales somewhere.

I leaned back in my chair and turned my glare up a notch. "I'll make some calls, but until we get a more precise location, there's not much I can do." I didn't like the idea of relying on a member of the public to call it in. Most mundanes – people without magical abilities – were all right rubbing shoulders with dwarves and elves but they got twitchy when monsters started walking down the street. That was where my team came in, trying to protect the balance between magical beings and mundanes without it devolving into a killing spree. But I didn't have the resources to send people on a wild manticore hunt across all of Wales.

"But–"

I held up my hand to stop the protest. "Do you know how big Wales is?"

"Do you?"

I gave the little one a half-point of grudging respect, but if he thought he could outmanoeuvre me, he was wrong.

"Maxi, how big is Wales?" I asked.

The young human blinked up at us from behind the pile of motherboards on his desk. He ran his hands through his blonde hair, causing it to stick up in a mad professor style that sat at odds with his youthful round face. "About twenty-one thousand square kilometres give or take."

I let out a low whistle. "Really?" That was big.

"Often used as a unit of land measurement because it's easily identifiable and–"

"Thank you, Maxi." I didn't want a speech on comparative country sizes, and Maxi was gearing up to a full-on lecture.

Turning back to the two sat in front of me, I said, "See. Unless you have the resources to survey that large an area…"

They hung their heads. They didn't have resources. If they did, they wouldn't have come to me.

I stood, intending to see them out when Dot appeared at my side in a blur of vampiric speed, a phone in her elegant hands.

"You're going to want to take this."

Frowning, I took the phone and listened to the breathless elf on the other side. I met the gaze of the two people still sitting at my desk.

"Looks like you're in luck. Someone's found a rogue manticore. We're going to Breconia."

~

The Breconian nature reserve wasn't too far from the human settlement of Brecon in Wales, but it had powerful magical shields to deter any mundanes that might wander in by accident and keep in the many dangerous creatures that lived there.

I parked the van with a screech of brakes in the huge carpark on the outskirts of the reserve. The elves made the excuse that modern vehicles couldn't go any further in case it upset the delicate balance of nature or something, but I didn't see them avoiding the internet or mobile phones.

Behind me, the two strangers who had given me fake names – John and James Doe. Come on. At least use some imagination – squirmed as they figured out how to undo their seatbelts. I frowned. There was something off about those two.

"Just click the red button. Haven't you used a seatbelt before?" I climbed out of the van and stretched, cracking my neck after hours of being cramped in the driver's seat. Dot stood by my side, surveying the green valley that stretched out below us at the foot of the cliffs that housed the carpark. The dark forest nestled right in the centre of the dip housed the elven city of Breconia.

"What do you make of them?"

"Heartbeats are a little faster than a human's, but that could be from your driving."

"There's nothing wrong with my driving. Anything else?" I trusted her vampire senses almost as much as my own, but she just shook her head.

"Something's weird. They didn't want the scarves."

I turned my snort into a cough. Thanks to her vampire speed and passion for crafts, Dot turned out knitwear like it was going out of fashion. If it had ever been in fashion. That sort of catwalk wasn't my thing; I stuck to business suits and sportswear. During the journey to Breconia, she'd whipped up a scarf for each of them, her needles having clacked in time with the nineties pop blaring out of the radio. They'd tried to refuse, but she'd pressed the woollen offerings into their hands with a toothy grin and they'd backed down, holding the scarves up at arm's length as they studied the knitting.

My phone beeped with an alert. It was Maxi – someone had to man the office and he was our best researcher – sending through all the research he had found on manticores. First mentioned in Persian myths, they had the body of a lion and the tail of a scorpion. They were about the size of a lion, and so on, nothing I didn't already know from a quick check of the magical species database. I closed the report as soon as I'd read the summary; I didn't need a twenty-page essay on manticore sub-species. Should be easy enough to catch it with the elves' help.

Our two guests managed to get out of the van. They now stood beside us, the scarves tied around their waists. Weird fashion statement, or did they not know what scarves were? I frowned. There was more to them than met the eye. But we had a manticore to track.

"Where is the manticore?" the taller one – I think it was James – asked.

I sighed. We were in elven territory now, had been ever since we had crossed through the magical barrier on the way to the carpark. I couldn't just waltz in and demand to speak to someone about the manticore. We had to wait for them to come to us. Even if they had invited us. Anything else and there could be an incident, and no one wanted to aggravate the elves. They had a good propaganda campaign thanks to a flurry of high fantasy stories in the twentieth century, but they lived for hundreds of years and could hold a grudge.

Above us, wings sounded, and the breeze brought the scent of big cat and bird crap to my nostrils. Sometimes my keen shifter senses were more of a curse than a blessing. Dot and I both tilted our necks so we could watch the elves approach. The other two copied us and I wasn't sure if they possessed supernatural senses too, or if they were trying to blend in.

The gryphons landed with a graceful thud on the packed earth of the carpark. A tall, slender elf slid off the first one. She was dressed in the golden uniform of the King's Guard, complete with helmet and sword. Her armour had several dents and a large scuff down the breastplate.

"Which one of you is Agent Jones?" she demanded.

I stepped forward. "I hear you've got a manticore problem."

"Captain Sylvana," the tall elf introduced herself. She gripped my forearm in a warrior's greeting. The gesture surprised me – elves normally bowed to strangers – but I returned it, testing her strength. We sized each other up for a moment before she released me. "I hope you're ready. This is like nothing I've seen before."

A fresh cut grazed her cheek, and her hand went to the scratch that dented the front of her green uniform.

"Show me."

"Mount up." The elf gestured to the gryphons and the half-eagle, half-lion creatures lay down at the command of their riders, so we could mount them.

I noticed the unease of the two strangers, but then riding a mythical creature wasn't an everyday occurrence. I should cut them some slack. Except, I didn't trust them as far as I could throw them. *Bad analogy*. I didn't trust them as far as Maxi could throw them.

Climbing onto a gryphon was simple, although my fitted suit stretched uncomfortably around my thighs. My cat instincts told me that I should be chasing this bird, not riding it, but I quashed that down. The elf mounted behind me and reached forward to grip the reins.

I opened my mouth to ask a question, but the wind stole the air from my throat as the gryphon ran over the edge of the cliff. A strangled yowl escaped my throat as we plummeted towards the emerald-green ground.

The gryphon's wings snapped open, and we slowed to a glide just before we hit the tops of the trees at the bottom of the valley. I gripped on tight as we flew towards the elven city of Breconia.

~

The gryphon touched down in an open landing space among the trees. Several paths meandered away from the clearing into a well-maintained forest. Any leaves had been swept to one side to keep the soft, mossy paths clear. The paths curved through the forest, gracefully carving a route around the trees. Shafts of sunlight beamed through the foliage, creating a pattern of light on the mossy floor. The trees themselves were huge. Red and brown wooden trunks reached towards the sky where a canopy of green and gold leaves shimmered in the breeze.

I half slipped, half staggered from the gryphon's back. Both my human and lynx halves were thankful to be back on solid ground. I resisted the urge to hug the moss-covered forest floor and instead straightened my suit and checked my bag was secure. Once I was sure I could speak without my voice wavering, I turned back to the elf.

"So, where's the manticore?"

The two men glanced round as if it would appear between the soaring trees at any second. They'd recovered from the flight faster than me. *Lucky dzrakers.*

"Follow me," the elf captain said, setting off towards the main, inhabited part of the city.

Winding staircases made of thick vines were twisted around each large trunk as we got closer to the city centre. Elves walked up and down the trees on different flights of steps and disappeared into the trees through doorways that looked like knots in the trunks. Vine bridges without handrails connected the trees together just below the canopy meaning that none of the elves had to touch the ground to go from one end of the city to another.

I walked just behind her, easily keeping up with her long strides. A small band of guards accompanied us, walking with the eerie silence that elves have perfected. Fear rolled off the civilian elves that scurried across the treetop walkways. A frown creased my forehead. Manticores were nasty, but an elf could avoid the creatures by climbing a tree.

"What's wrong with them?"

The elf guard eyed the citizens. "Just wait 'til you see."

"See what?"

"This." The captain stopped abruptly, and I walked into her back.

Utter destruction lay before us. I stepped into the centre and took it in. A sharp tang curled my nostril hairs, the stench was like lion's piss only worse. The manticore had scented this place. I moved to a tree that leaned at an angle; it was out of place in the neat, curated elven forest. I ran my hand along a claw mark, etched deep into the wood.

Large splinters littered the ground along with scraps of clothing. A smear of blood darkened the pale trunk of another tree, and the metallic tang of it fought with the manticore's scent mark. My teeth lengthened as my fighting instincts kicked in, an automatic response to danger.

I took a moment to get back under control. "It killed someone?"

Sylvana nodded, her face a grim mask of grief. "A civilian."

"A manticore did this?" Disbelief laced my voice. Manticores weren't much bigger than a lion, even if they were a lot more dangerous. There was no way they could knock over an enchanted tree.

"It was like nothing I've ever seen. Huge, half as big as one of our home trees, and–" She swallowed. "It had wings."

"Then it wasn't a manticore." I folded my arms. "I need to know what we're dealing with. Has one of your gryphons gone rogue?"

Even as I said it, I knew I was wrong. Gryphons didn't get that big.

She marched over to me, invading my personal space. The elf pushed my shoulder. "I know what a gryphon looks like. This wasn't it. It's nothing I've seen in the forest before."

That was saying something. The elven reserve of Breconia that surrounded their city was home to all sorts of creatures.

"Alright, we'll figure this out." I held my hands up in a placating gesture. Sylvana backed up. "Let's go hunt a manticore or whatever this thing is."

~

We tracked the trail of destruction away from the inhabited part of the city and into the surrounding forest. The further we got from the dwellings, the wilder the woods became, as manicured topiary and perfectly spaced trees gave way to the chaos of nature.

An elven arrow stuck out of a gnarled oak tree. I sniffed. More blood. My fingers twitched over the standard issue crossbow I'd strapped to my thigh. Standard issue for the Magical Liaison Office, it could cope with most magical threats with the ash bolts tipped with silver, it usually gave me comfort, but hearing about the size of this thing…I longed for something more high-powered.

"Was this the manticore too?" I whispered, the closeness of the forest making me more aware of the predators that lurked within. It wasn't just rogue manticores that roamed the wilds of the Breconian nature reserve.

The captain nodded.

"What happened?"

"We decided we needed help." Anger flashed across her face. Elven pride didn't easily allow for outside help. Things were bad.

"How many did you lose?"

"Five of my best. I was lucky to get away with a flesh wound." She kept her gaze straight ahead. "Others weren't so lucky."

I swore under my breath before turning to survey our troops; a handful of elves, me and Dot. We needed more backup. A shifter and a vampire counted for a lot, but if this thing had taken out a band of elite elven warriors, then we were in trouble. And I didn't think I could rely on the two weird men in a fight.

I sniffed the air and followed its scent to a stream that flowed around the clearing, innocently gurgling through the forest.

The manticore's potent stench disappeared into the water. Dzrak. My gaze rested on the two strangers staring across the stream, and I strode over. Time for some answers.

The large one turned to look at me an instant before I slammed him back against a tree. The silver bracelet flew off his hand at the impact. "What the hell is this thing?"

"M…manticore," he gasped, his throat tight under my forearm. Then he garbled some made-up words I couldn't understand.

"Don't mock me."

The smaller man placed his hand on my shoulder. "Let him go."

The compulsion made me step back before I realised what had happened. I whirled round and faced the little guy, my teeth bared and my hands shaking as I fought to control my anger and stop the shift rippling through me.

"Don't ever use compulsion on me again."

A crossbow clicked.

"Want me to hit them somewhere it hurts?" Dot asked in a singsong voice, as if she was chatting about the weather or her latest crochet project.

I raised an eyebrow at the two strangers. "Your move."

The taller one swallowed hard, beads of sweat trickling down his forehead. The smaller one, John, sighed. "Enough. It is a manticore."

I opened my mouth, but he held up a hand to stop my outburst.

"I swear it, but…it is not of your realm."

"What the dzrak does that mean?"

Another sigh. "I cannot tell you everything."

I stepped forward again. These secrets were going to get us killed.

"Who are you?"

"We are merely servants. All I can say is that it escaped. It is larger and stronger than the manticores you have here. We were sent here to retrieve it…" He plucked at the gold bracelet on his wrist. "You can leave if you so desire. We will handle the manticore." John swallowed again and James looked like he might faint.

I inhaled deeply. "Like dzrak you will. This is under my jurisdiction. People have been hurt. I'm seeing this through."

"And I," chimed in the captain, "I will not have you risk elven lives if you fail."

"I'm in too," Dot said, smiling so we could see her fangs.

"Now that that's over with…" I stopped. A thumping sound came from the forest. I spun round, my crossbow aimed towards the noise. "We've got company."

The wait felt like an eternity but was, in reality, less than a minute. All of us tensed, ready to face an otherworldly manticore.

Out of the corner of my eye, a flash of silver shone between John's hands. He had conjured a net of spider-thin silk. I hoped he knew what he was doing, because that thing didn't look like it could hold a fish, let alone a rampaging manticore.

Hairy legs burst through the trees. Ten of them. Not a manticore, but a hideous tarfangtula. The oversized spider creatures that lurked in the nature reserve resembled a red-kneed tarantula. If the spider had ten legs, ten globular eyes and was bigger than a pony.

Everybody froze.

"What are the odds it's passing through?" Dot said out of the corner of her mouth.

It's ten bulbous eyes focused on our party. Unable to pass up free food, it lunged for the closest elf.

"I think that answers your question."

I shot off crossbow bolts, aiming for its bulging eyes and was rewarded with a screech of pain and yellow gunk running down its ugly face.

The spider-like nightmare lashed out, its fangs clacking at elves as they darted in, their blades flashing to cut its bristling legs.

Clicking sparked off in the surrounding forest. More tarfangtulas crashed into the clearing.

I shouted a warning as they surrounded us.

Clawed legs towered above us, half the height of the enormous trees that soared towards the sky. I dodged as one came down where I had stood.

Dot snatched a blade from a fallen elf and dashed around the clearing with vampiric speed, hacking at their tough legs. I shouted and waved to draw their attention before firing off another crossbow bolt at the nearest one.

The two men, or whatever they were, from another realm backed up against a tree, holding up their net as if something that flimsy could protect them.

Sylvana had her elves well trained. Using their superior agility, they weaved among the monsters, hacking, and shouting.

I spotted the pattern. They wanted to drive the creatures away without more injury. Dzraking elves and their respect for life. All well and good, until you were up against fae abominations that wanted to kill you.

Dodging legs and aiming my crossbow, I made my way to the captain.

That horrible clacking came again as the tarfangtulas clicked their mandibles together in some spider language. Those that could move, ran into the forest, disappearing into the shadows of the trees. A pathetic, half-dead tarfangtula dragged its oozing body across the ground in a desperate attempt to reach its comrades. I put it out of its misery.

"Why did they just leave?" Sylvana asked, looking around the clearing in confusion.

"Almost like they were afraid of something…" The words died on my lips as a gigantic creature leapt through the undergrowth.

The musky scent of male lion mixed with sulphur filled my nose, and my eyes watered as I choked on the stench. As I blinked back tears, I took in the huge cat.

Cat was an understatement. This monster was bigger than a van, bigger than the enormous tarfangtulas which had fled just moments ago. It was dzraking huge.

It had the tawny body and head of a lion on steroids, with a bushy red mane sprouting from its neck. Its fur ended at the base of its tail, where it faded into dark scales with crimson spikes dotted along the ridges. The spikes grew larger as they reached the pointed end where an enormous scorpion stinger pulsed. Two gigantic blood-red wings sprouted from its back, tucked against its golden-brown fur.

It growled as it saw us, and its cat body shuffled, preparing to pounce.

I yelled a warning, recognising the behaviour all too well.

The manticore leapt, pinning an elf with its massive paws, crushing the armour as if it were cloth.

I loaded a silver-tipped bolt, careful to avoid the stinging metal, and aimed my crossbow at its head. It moved at the last second and the arrow grazed its skin. But it was enough.

The creature whipped round, its tail up, ready to strike. I readied another bolt, fired, then rolled as it pounced towards me.

Not fast enough. The tips of its claws grazed my arm, drawing blood as it cut through my jacket. *Dzrak. This was a good suit.*

Dot zipped forward, sword in hand. It growled and swatted her with one paw. The manticore's claws closed in.

Dzrak this.

The change rippled through me as I shifted into my lynx form, my clothes and crossbow disappearing into the magic of the change. The sudden shift heightened my senses, and I sneezed as the manticore's sharp scent hit the back of my throat.

I leapt at the creature, landing partway up one of its huge hind legs. I clawed my way to its back. It yowled at the pain and whirled round to shake me off.

I sank my teeth into its rump, the taste of bad eggs and fresh blood filling my mouth along with its thick fur. It howled with pain and reared up. I jumped and clawed through the thin membrane of its wings. At least now it couldn't fly out of here.

My ears twitched at a change in air pressure, and I released my grip, dodging to the side as its tail stabbed down, venom dripping from its scorpion stinger. This close, I could see the dark red bristles that dotted its pulsing poison sac.

I jumped down, landing lightly on the mossy ground.

The elves had formed a circle around the creature, aiming to contain it.

Dot was back in the action, joining the elves, her sword up, looking for a place to strike.

The two men had their net ready, approaching it from behind, speaking softly as if the manticore was a stray dog they needed to calm.

It reacted to their voices.

But not how they wanted.

Instead of calming the manticore, their soft tones enraged it. Its slitted yellow eyes narrowed, and it spun round, lashing out with its tail and knocking them to the ground. The net flew from their hands, landing in grass damp with yellow tarfangtula blood.

The men's bodies sprawled across the ground. I hoped they were unconscious and not dead.

No time to check.

Enraged, the manticore leapt over the elves, spun round, and swiped two away. I ran in while it was distracted and launched myself at its softer underbelly, raking my claws into its furred skin before darting away.

The captain stabbed at its flank, using her elven agility to jump gracefully over its dangerous tail as it jabbed at her. A drop of acid green venom dripped onto her arm, and she yelped as her armour started smoking.

Don't let the poison touch you. Good to know.

I darted over to her and pulled her out of reach of its tail with my teeth. She panted hard and muttered her thanks as she got back to her feet and transferred her sword to her other hand.

Gritting her perfect teeth, she ran back in, rallying the rest of her team with a cry. "To me!"

I joined her, and Dot appeared at my side in a blur of speed. One full frontal assault. We could do this.

The manticore faced our small team, planting its feet as it stared them down. With a roar, it breathed out searing hot flames at the elven captain. I knocked her aside, sending her sprawling on the ground.

The stench of singed fur caught my nostrils as someone shoved into me.

I skidded across the clearing, roaring my grief as Dot's pale skin blistered under its fiery assault. She fell to the ground.

Now it's personal. No one lays into my team except me.

Roaring my defiance, I darted in again and again, using the adrenaline spiking through me to avoid its attacks.

The elf captain was back on her feet, stabbing at its furred head to distract it while I carried out my assault. It swiped with one massive paw.

A scream cut through the air. The captain flew across the glade, thudding into a tree. She didn't get up.

Dzrak this. We hadn't slowed the manticore at all, despite the flesh wounds we'd given it. And even in my lynx form, I was no match for an oversized lion with a dzraking poison tail.

A flash of silver caught my eye. The net. That was how I could end this.

I shifted back to my human form, rolled to avoid its spiked tail, and picked up the net. My hands burned on contact with the flimsy material. *Dzrak it. Why does it have to be silver?*

I gripped it more tightly, the knotted squares scorching my skin with cold as every instinct told me to drop it and get as far away from the evil metal as I could.

But I dealt with close contact to silver every day. The metal tipped my crossbow bolts for a reason; it was effective against most supernaturals. That didn't mean I had to like it.

Panting hard, I shifted into my lynx form, letting out a roar of pain as the silver merged with my magic, burning into the change, making it a hundred times worse than normal. I staggered as the silver clouded my mind. I shook my head and fought to think straight.

The manticore reared up, its claws flashing in the dappled light that shone between the forest leaves.

I leapt.

I landed on its furred back and dug in my claws. The creature roared out in pain and whirled around, trying to shake me. I crawled forward, inching my way along its massive body, my teeth gritted against the pain of silver. I had one shot at this.

I reached its neck. Its thick, greasy mane got in my mouth, choking me. It shook its head, rattling my brain. I hung on.

It lunged forward, aiming to scratch me off with a tree. *This was it.*

I shifted to my human form. The agony of the shift while holding silver sent spots of white light across my vision and stole my breath. I pressed the net against its skin as it collided with the tree, sending me sprawling down the trunk.

But the net did its work.

It expanded, fuelled by whatever magic it contained, wrapping the manticore's head in the light silvered webbing.

The manticore roared in frustration, then whimpered and sank to the ground, clawing weakly at its restraint as it fought a yawn. *What sort of knock-out magic was this?* The net grew again, trapping its front paws before snaking up its body and entangling every inch of the huge creature from its nose to its wicked spiked tail. The manticore didn't mind; it had already fallen asleep and innocent snores huffed from its wet nose.

I pushed myself up from the floor. Every part of me sang in pain. The impact with the tree and the silver had taken its toll even on my quick healing body. I might have to take the weekend off to recover. I snarled at the thought.

John and James stepped forward, looking ruffled but otherwise no worse for wear. Either they had strong glamour, or they were tougher than they looked.

John walked up to me. He said something in a language I didn't understand, and his human form wavered, revealing a tiny demon complete with forked tail. I blinked. But he was back to his usual self. *How hard did I hit my head?*

He adjusted the bangles at his wrist and when he next spoke, his words were in English.

"Thank you." He held out his hand.

I stared at him, but shook it, enjoying his slight wince as I squeezed with my shifter strength. Yes, it was petty, but I wasn't sorry.

Behind us, James conjured a sparkling portal that swirled with a black so dark it sucked the light from the clearing.

"You have a favour from Hades should you ever be in need of it."

I started to ask who the dzrak Hades was, because they couldn't mean the god of the Underworld, but they had grabbed the net and disappeared through the portal before I could ask the question.

Forming a fist, I thumped the tree and groaned as pain lanced through me. I scanned the forest for my teammate and found Dot curled on the ground. I hurried over, half crouched, half limping, my teeth clenched.

It was impossible to tell if she was alive. Her vampire skin was badly burned, but cool to the touch; vampire pulses were so slow I couldn't use that as an indicator. There was only one way to know for sure. Holding my breath, I brought my forearm in front of her face and let blood fall from the open wound onto her lips.

Her tongue flicked out, licking my blood. Dot lunged forward with inhuman speed and plunged her fangs into my arm. I winced at the initial pain before the anaesthetising effect of her saliva took over. At least my arm didn't hurt anymore. When she opened her eyes, I knew she was alright.

My head swam. "That's enough, Dot."

Her eyes flashed red, but she withdrew her fangs and licked the wound, helping it to close. "You taste like wet cat."

"You're alive then."

"Just give me a week's leave to recover. That should be sufficient."

I snorted out a laugh. "You can have a day."

She sighed and lay back down. "Fair enough."

The captain of the elven guard blinked and rubbed her forehead as she used a tree to prop herself upright. She lifted her sword. "Where is it? What happened?"

I filled her in. her eyes widened when I got to the part about the portal but she kept silent until I'd finished.

"That was…something," she said.

"Yup."

Sylvana grimaced as she stared around the clearing. "My team…"

Dot answered. "All heartbeats are stable. If you've got a healer, I suggest you start with that one." She pointed at a prone elf lying crumpled on the ground. "He's lost a lot of b–" She took a deep breath before she finished the word, forcing it between her fangs like it had done her a personal wrong. "Blood."

The captain called it in and soon a band of elven healers appeared, their green, soothing magic filling the clearing with the scent of fresh-cut grass. One of them offered to heal me. I considered brushing them away, but the scorching sting of silver still scoured my skin, so I accepted and only sneezed twice as the unfamiliar magic brushed against my shifter healing abilities, making me woozy.

I pinched the bridge of my nose. "I need a drink."

Sylvana smiled, her elven hearing picking up my whisper. "I can help with that."

She slipped a carved hip flask out from somewhere under her armour. "I always carry it. For emergencies."

The elf handed me the bottle, and I sipped, coughing as the harsh liquid burned its way down my throat. "Fire whisky?" I croaked.

She shrugged and took the flask back, taking a drink herself. "Sometimes honey mead just doesn't cut it."

The elf went up in my estimation. "You're not so bad…for an elf."

"You're not so bad yourself…for a shifter."

~

Back at the office, I sank into my chair, enjoying the familiar smell of musty books and old leather.

"How'd it go?" asked Maxi as he brought me my coffee; black and strong. Just how I liked it.

"Weird." He gave me a look and I amended my answer. "Weirder than normal."

"And Dot?"

"She's got the rest of the day off."

Maxi let out a whistle. He knew things were bad when I let the team take unscheduled leave. Normally, we needed all hands on deck just to keep up with the dzraking paperwork.

I took a swig of my coffee, savouring the bitter taste. "Any fires I should know about back here?"

He coughed. "Funny you should mention that…" Maxi placed a report on my desk. I scanned the first page. Some idiot witch with a pyromaniac complex. With a sigh, I downed my coffee and reholstered my crossbow. Just another day in the Magical Liaison Office.

Mermaid Quay

The dead body in the water wasn't a good start to my day. Or his.

When Agent Jones is called out to a mermaid murder, she realises there's more going on that meets the eye. Can she solve the crime and stop the killings or is she in too deep?

This is a never before published story that came from a writing prompt about mermaids. Enjoy!

I looked down at the body floating in the murky waters of Cardiff Bay. Not a good start to my day. Or his.

A couple of police officers on a marked speedboat pulled the man aboard with as much care as if he were a sack of potatoes and headed for the shore. I sighed and walked down to meet them. Dzrak, I hated water.

"Second one this week," Dot said, falling into step next to me. The vampire pulled her chunky knit jumper tight against her body as we approached the jetty.

"It might not be a supernatural killing." I tried to keep the edge of hope out of my voice. If it was a standard murder, it wouldn't be part of the Magical Liaison Office's jurisdiction and that meant it would be somebody else's problem.

"Police personnel only, Miss," a young policeman said, as he stepped forward to head us off.

I flicked open my leather wallet and showed him my badge. "Agent Jones. Magical Liaison Office. You called me."

He backed off. Dealing with me was above his paygrade. Good. I'd only been in the city a couple of months; my reputation must be spreading fast. After a whispered conversation, a man in a badly fitted suit hurried over.

"Thank goodness you're here." I arched an eyebrow, unused to having the police happy to see me. "It looks like it's the same as the drowning on Saturday. We've got eyewitnesses claiming they saw something in the water. Something unnatural."

I understood. He was glad we were there because now it was my problem.

"Let's see the body first. I don't want to investigate a drunk who fell in."

The detective nodded and led the way down to the wooden jetty where the officers in the boat had laid the corpse on its back.

I knelt by the body, my sensitive nose wrinkling at the sharp smell of salt and dead fish with an undertone of decomposition. He'd been in the water all night. I borrowed the detective's pen and pushed back the fashionable jacket. And sighed.

There, slashed across his chest through the plain white t-shirt, were the claw marks of a mermaid. I swore. It was definitely my problem.

Dot came up behind me and pulled a face. "The water's washed away most of the blood but I'd say he died before midnight."

"You can tell that just by looking at him?" the detective asked.

Dot met his gaze, her normally dull red eyes glowed for an instant. "Something like that."

The detective backed away. Vampires tended to have that effect on people. Mind you, so did I.

I stood and pinched the bridge of my nose, trying to think. I let my gaze trail across the calm waters, taking in the glass-fronted restaurants. Jutting out into the bay, construction work had started on a new boutique hotel. I didn't know much about mermaids, but they'd been swimming happily in the waters around Britain for thousands of years, so why the sudden murders?

I took some pictures with my phone. Regardless of motive, I'd do my best to get justice for the victims and their families. I jerked my head towards Dot. It was time we took a walk. She nodded back and pulled on her oversized sun hat and the sunglasses that made her look like an insect. That was the problem with a vampire employee, they couldn't be in direct sunlight without some serious sunblock.

I growled involuntarily as I spotted the man in the sharp suit approach. The last thing I needed was the mayor getting involved. I hated politics. I tried to slink off, but he hailed me after a moment's consultation with the detective.

"Agent Jones?"

I fixed a bright smile on my face and turned back. The smell of his aftershave almost overpowered my shifter senses. "Mayor Taf. What brings you out from your office this early in the morning?"

He blinked, then smiled, showing off his shining white teeth. "Actually, you do. Or rather, this case does."

I frowned in confusion.

"These murders are making everyone jumpy. We need to make sure that the killer is brought to justice so people can feel safe again. They're talking about delaying the building work and the press is having a field day with the supernatural serial killer–"

"Not a serial killer."

"Pardon?" I took some pleasure in noting that he couldn't quite frown. I guess the rumours about his Botox habit were true.

"Technically, you need three murders to class the culprit as a serial killer."

He raked his hand through his greying blonde hair. "Yes, well, I'm sure you have it all in hand, but I hardly need to tell you how precarious the tension between humans and supernaturals is..." I stared at him. Of course I knew that. It was part of my job to know. "Just catch them quickly, alright Jones?"

I nodded curtly. He strode off, giving a jaunty wave to a couple of joggers as he stepped into his chauffeur driven car.

Once he had left, I motioned to Dot to follow me. She yawned as we climbed the steps back up to the pedestrian walkway. Only a couple more hours and she'd fall asleep on the job. Vampires were great on the night shift, but not so much in the daytime. We needed to get some more employees in the Cardiff branch.

I inhaled deeply, allowing the salty air to clear my nostrils after the stench of the mayor's aftershave and the rotting smell of the day-old corpse. The tantalising smell of frying bacon wafted across the bay, making me drool. It was early morning, and most of the restaurants in the regenerated area known as Mermaid Quay were closed, but, as in most British cities, there was always one café serving up a cooked breakfast so thick with grease that you could get a heart attack just by looking at it.

"Can you sense anything?" Dot interrupted my thoughts.

I turned my back on the promise of a doorstop sandwich and leaned against the metal railings that stopped tourists from falling into the dark water. I scanned the water then turned back to the gentrified area of restaurants, letting my shifter senses take it all in. To the other side of the bay, builders shouted as they worked on site.

"Nothing." I shook my head. "Why now? What's happened in the last week that's made a mermaid kill two people?"

Dot shrugged. "Maybe one of them has gone wild. It happens."

"Maybe…" Supernaturals were more similar to humans that people thought in that regard; they could go on a crazy killing spree at the drop of a hat, the same as anyone could. But this felt different. Two young men murdered in the late evening, both with ashy blonde hair and medium builds. It felt more targeted.

I turned to Dot. "Why don't you go get some sleep while I call in some tech support?"

Maxi smiled as he walked over. We'd worked together in the London office; I'd trained him up and he was always happy to lend me a hand in investigations. He shook my hand warmly, ran his hand through his messy hair until it stuck up on end, and set down his black rucksack carefully on the paved walkway.

"You mentioned mermaids, what?"

I smiled back, used to his public schoolboy accent and strange way of talking. I nodded towards the bay. "In there. I need to know what's down there."

Maxi nodded, unphased by my request. He rifled through his backpack and retrieved a black device with a large screen and two antennas sticking out from it like some sort of weird bug.

"What is it?" I asked.

"It's one of the Office's latest tech projects, I worked on it personally. It's utterly fascinating. You see, we've been able to modify all types of tech to focus on supernaturals –"

"Maxi…" I cut him off before he could launch into a lecture about the latest research projects that melded magic with technology.

"Oh, yah, well it's a type of SONAR device, tuned into magical signatures. It can't pick up on the type of magical being, but if there's anything down there with magic, this bad boy will find it." He swung the cable. "I need to get closer to the water for it to work."

I led the way down the stone steps back to the jetty where a corpse had lain a couple of hours earlier. Maxi bent down and stretched towards the water. I had a vision of him plunging into the deceptively calm waters, so I reached forward and gripped his shoulder.

"Don't fall in!"

Maxi laughed up at me. "Don't worry about me! One time, on a school trip to Lake Como, our teacher thought it would be a laugh to make us swim fully clothed across the lake! Of course, he didn't realise we'd snuck some drinks in the night before. It was carnage! Anthony actually chundered partway across! Anyway, I've just got to get this into the bay and then I've linked up the screen with this tablet, yah, so you can watch on there."

He handed me the thin device, already loaded to mirror the smaller green screen on the SONAR scanner. Currently, it only showed concentric circles in neon green with a lazy line that swept around the screen. I touched my magic dampening bracelet self-consciously, wondering if that was the only thing preventing the gadget from picking up my shifter signature.

I watched him carefully as he lowered the scanner into the water then he stood, gently winding out the black cable that linked it to the tablet. We both peered down at the blinking tablet.

A loud beep made me jump. I silently cursed my sensitive ears and watched the screen. A round blip had appeared on the edge of the SONAR's range.

"There!" said Maxi unnecessarily.

I ignored him. More bleeps sounded and my eyes widened as more and more round dots filled the screen. I looked up, across the bay. Nothing. But under the surface, it teemed with supernatural creatures.

"Are they all mermaids?" I asked.

"No way to tell for sure without going in, but I read up on them on the train here." Of course he did. "It's fascinating, what! We know they live in large family groups and they're very territorial and, excellent swimmers…"

"Maxi."

"…but they don't seem to like living too close to humans. If there's really a school of mermaids in Cardiff Bay, they should be protected yah…"

"Maxi! What does that mean?" I pointed at the screen where three of the blips had surged away from the others.

His blue eyes widened. "It looks like some are coming this way…" The blips jolted into the inner circle. "But, that's impossible! The speed!" The bleeps were almost continuous. We both looked up at the water.

Then the noise stopped. I hit the side of the tablet with the palm of my hand. Maxi grabbed it off me. I tapped my foot on the wooden jetty and stared at the water. I took a step back as a dark shape surged underneath the surface, then disappeared.

"It's not the tablet…" He pulled up the cable and gaped at the cut wire. "They've taken the scanner."

I swore, venting some frustration in Dwarfish; the best language to swear in. Maxi typed up his findings in the tablet and replayed the SONAR scan, which he had recorded.

"Looks like there's at least a dozen, but they keep moving so it's hard to be precise – they're all grouped together."

"But why are they killing people? What do they want?"

Maxi shrugged and pulled his fingers through his light blonde hair, making it stick up in all directions like a mad professor. "If only we could ask them…"

I grinned. "Great idea."

~

"I'm just walking down the promenade, your everyday chap just walking in the evening."

I groaned and hissed at Maxi through the earpiece, "Stop talking to yourself and act natural."

"Well forgive me, but I need to get into character! I didn't get selected to play Juliet in our school production by improvising!"

"Maybe you should try walking along the pier and getting a coffee." Dot's smooth voice interrupted our bickering.

Maxi squared his shoulders and headed for the coffee stand with affected nonchalance. "Good day, my man, one cup of hot java beans please!"

I pressed a button and disconnected Maxi from my earbud. "This is never going to work."

"Have some faith," Dot said and gave me a wave from her position on the quay.

I stretched out on the bench a little further along the walkway. It was nine o'clock and the sun had disappeared over the horizon, leaving the sky a murky yellow. I tapped my foot as we waited. An hour passed and the restaurant goers started to leave in clouds of merriment, leaving me and my team and those who were out for drinks. A group of four lads weaved their way along the pier to where Maxi leant against the railing.

One of them climbed up and began a mock tightrope walk along the balustrade. I huffed out a sigh and made to get up when his scream ripped through the air.

I ran. Through the railings, I could see clawed hands wrapped around the man's legs. His friends shouted in fear and confusion. Maxi had grabbed his wrist and held on, grunting at the strain. I opened my mouth to shout for Dot, but the vampire was already there. With a blur of speed, she appeared next to Maxi and reached for the civilian's other wrist. Between them, they heaved and pulled the man back onto the pier before I'd even stepped foot on the slatted wooden boards. But the man wasn't alone.

The mermaid had kept hold and was now on the decking, hissing and shrieking as it squirmed. It was larger than I'd expected, at least eight feet long from the tip of its tail to its head. Partway up its midriff, the rubbery dolphin-like tail dissolved into wet skin. Dot shoved the man into his friends and compelled them to run with a blast of her vampiric powers. I sprinted forward, drawing the standard issue crossbow from my thigh holster.

"Stop or I'll shoot!"

The half-fish creature ignored me and lunged for Maxi. Dot yanked him out of the way. I swore and dropped the crossbow. I jumped and shifted into my lynx form in mid-air.

I landed on the creature with a thud and sank my claws into its slippery body. This close, the smell of seaweed and raw fish filled my nostrils. It screamed in pain and wriggled, trying to buck me off. It thrashed its powerful tail. I tried to ignore the wet of its clammy skin against my fur. It was strong, but I held on, pinning it down with my bulky lynx body. I grunted out a roar and Dot appeared at my side, her own crossbow in her hand.

"You are under arrest," she said.

The mermaid's deep green eyes focused on the pointed end of an arrow, and it raised its hands over its head in a gesture of surrender.

"Justice. Please. Justice!" The mermaid said in a thick accent that reminded me of foam capped waves. It looked up at me with pleading eyes. "He killed my baby, our young…"

I tilted my head to one side and retracted my claws. She stayed still, watching me through strands of murky green hair. I took a breath and shifted. The pain of the shift rocked me for a second, but I fought through it and stared down at the mermaid, now pinned between my thighs in my human form.

"What do you mean he killed your young?"

"Him!" The creature glared at Maxi, now approaching carefully.

"Maxi? Impossible."

"Who is Maxi?" asked the mermaid, her turquoise brow crinkling.

"Yah?"

This was getting out of hand. I pinched the bridge of my nose and asked again. "Who killed your children?"

The mermaid narrowed her green eyes at Maxi and hissed out a name. "Him. Taf."

"As in Mayor Taf?"

The sea creature nodded. "His building crushed our school. Ten of our young killed."

I followed her gaze to the partially built floating hotel on the other side of the bay.

"Why didn't you report this?"

"Report it to who?"

"The Magical Liaison Office."

"You work with him!"

"That isn't the mayor!"

The mermaid squinted, then shrugged. "All you land goers look the same to us. Besides, the great Lir did not command it."

"Who's Lir?"

"Our leader."

"Can I get an audience with Lir?"

"I can ask…if you let me go."

I weighed up my options. On the one hand, the mermaid had attacked someone but, on the other, humans had possibly killed ten kids. In the end, there was only one choice I could make.

"Alright, but if I don't hear back from you in an hour, my team will have to come down."

The mermaid arched one eyebrow, but she nodded. I got up and watched her use her powerful arms to lift her body over the railings. She dived into the water in a curving arc that didn't even leave a ripple on the surface.

~

The meeting was set for midnight. I had called in one of our magic users to spell me with protection wards and told the others to stay back as I waited at the end of the jetty. The crescent moon reflected on the glass black sea like a drowning egg.

The salt water frothed and bubbled less than two feet from where I stood. I planted my feet on the boards and crossed my arms. The water writhed until it looked like dark snakes sliding across the surface. With a burst of speed, a huge merman surged out of the depths.

He was naked from the waist up and the water dripped from his imposing muscular chest. His eyes were level with mine as he used his tail to tread water. He held a spear fashioned from some sort of grey rock, spikes glinting in the twinkling lights from the restaurant quarter.

"Lir?"

He inclined his head. I noted the coral pink crown twined into his long black hair. It contrasted oddly with his blue-green skin.

"Agent Jones." I held out my hand. He looked at it then back to me. I put it back at my side. "I want to help."

His eyes narrowed. "Your people have killed our younglings. I demand retribution."

"And one of your mermaids has killed two men."

He nodded sadly. "I know, I have seen to it that Nerissa will harm no others. But she is in mourning for her son and the nine other younglings killed."

"I need to see it for myself. Can you guarantee the safety of a dive team?"

"If you need to see the devastation, I can take you now."

I scoffed. "I can't breathe underwater."

"Easily remedied." The huge merman waved his arms and a giant bubble emerged from the softly lapping waves. It bobbed straight for me. I held out my arms. Nope. No way was I getting in that thing. I backed up a step.

"I don't think—"

It surrounded me, cutting off my words. I pressed on the sides of the bubble, but it solidified into something that felt like slimy jelly. Dot ran forward. With a flick of his wrist, Lir directed the bubble to his side.

"Now you will see."

He dived into the depths. Dot stared after me, mouthing something I couldn't hear as the bubble sank below the surface. I clenched my fists and met her gaze for as long as I could.

Underwater, the silvery moonlight played just below the surface and the bright lights from the streetlamps allowed me to orientate myself. Not that I had any control over where I was going.

The bubble followed the merman at breakneck speed across the bay and I had to concentrate to stay upright as it sped along. We headed deeper and the lights above us faded into a distant promise.

"I can't see anything down here."

Lir ignored me and I strained my shifter senses. It was too dark, and the bubble dampened my keen hearing. I shuddered. This must be how humans feel all the time.

The bubble slowed and I pressed against its slimy side, trying to see where we were. A dull, blue light shone straight ahead. As we approached it, I realised it wasn't just one light, it was many small, glowing rocks and they illuminated neat rows of seaweed. Farms, I realised. And coral gardens. And a group of mermaids. They darted around my bubble, jostling it and sending it spiralling. I fell backwards, desperately seeking purchase on the jelly-like surface.

Lir spoke in his underwater language. It sounded like a calm song, and they stopped torturing me. Instead, they all turned to watch me, their dark eyes dark hostile as they swam back a little to allow us to pass.

Lir stopped suddenly, beating his tail to keep still in the water. He stared straight ahead. I followed his gaze, and my bubble drifted closer. It was devastating. Crushed coral littered the seabed next to huge rocks. Grey particles floated through the blue light, not yet settled on the sea floor.

"What happened here?"

"It was an ordinary day. This was where our younglings gathered to learn and play. There was a cave that kept them sheltered even in the deepest storm. There was no warning. Bright lights and shockwaves came, and before we knew what had happened, the cave was destroyed and there was rubble everywhere. And the school was gone. Ten younglings dead, and two teachers buried with them. Nerissa was one of the mothers. She should not have killed humans to atone for this, but perhaps I should have acted sooner." His tone shifted from sadness to anger. "So, I have decided. You have until the next moonrise to bring me justice or I will call down a wave to drown this city."

I wanted to go closer, and the bubble responded, bobbing towards the destruction. I took pictures with my phone, not knowing if the soft light was enough. I considered the rocks. They weren't all natural. I reached my hand forward, wanting to take a piece of the concrete I had spotted. And the bubble burst.

My fingers closed around my prize and then I kicked upwards, panic overtaking me. The merfolk wouldn't let me drown, would they? I was their only hope of justice without being destroyed. I kicked harder, my lungs burning with the effort of not breathing.

I breached the surface and gulped down sweet oxygen. I struck out for the nearest steps. Dzrak, I hated water.

Cold and shaking, I clambered to land and looked out across the calm surface of the bay. I gripped the concrete in my hand and my mind raced. The mermaid had said Taf had killed them, why was she so sure? I eyed the concrete before my gaze raised to the building works towering over the water. I shook my head, sending droplets flying from my sodden hair. I needed a drink. Whatever the mermaid meant, it would have to wait until morning.

~

I waited just outside the building site, coffee in hand, before the first builders arrived. Beside me, Maxi bobbed up and down at my side, checking his man bag every thirty seconds to make sure his gadgets hadn't wandered off since he last checked. I watched a group of workers enter the site, binned my coffee cup and headed in. Maxi jogged to keep up.

"You can't be here!"

I flashed my badge at the man scurrying towards me with a clipboard in his meaty hands. He eyed it, then me.

"What do you want?"

"There was an explosion last week."

"And? It was all sanctioned by the city and we put up the safety notices. It was all done by the book. No one was hurt."

My jaw tightened. "Ten mer-children were killed plus two teachers."

He scoffed. "Mermaids? Pull the other one."

I stepped forward and he retreated until his back pressed against the chain link security fence. "I don't think you want me angry. So, here's what's going to happen; you are going to get me everything you have on this building and who authorised what and, if you're lucky you'll only get charged with manslaughter and neglect instead of murder."

He swallowed, his Adam's apple bobbing up and down.

"Nod if you agree."

He nodded. I backed off and smiled. "Good. Now take Maxi here to your office, he loves looking through paperwork."

~

At five p.m. sharp, I was down at the mayor's office, a thick file in my hand courtesy of Maxi and a few favours. The waiting area was a byword for excess with plush red carpet and gold panels lining the walls. I scowled, instantly distrusting the Victorian signs of authority.

"I need to see the mayor."

"Do you have an appointment?" His lean secretary made a game attempt at formality.

"He asked me to keep him up to date on the case down the Bay."

Maxi put a warning hand on my shoulder. I backed up a step. It wasn't the secretary's fault – he was doing his job. Just like me.

The secretary eyed me nervously and put in a call.

The mayor came out and led me through to his office. Oil paintings of previous mayors in their ceremonial garb lined the walls and a large antique desk filled most of one side of the room.

He gestured to the plump chairs on the other side. I sank into one and Maxi took another. I dropped the manila folder onto the round table in front of us. The mayor eyed it and rubbed his hands together.

"How's the investigation coming along, got any progress for me?"

"Yes," I smiled. "I've found out why Nerissa was killing people."

"Then you know who did it? Excellent."

"I do. She's being kept in custody by their leader, Lir."

He frowned, his brows managing to move together by a couple of millimetres despite the toxins that froze his face. "I was expecting a more public form of justice, to reassure the people, but I suppose it's good that she's been caught and won't be a danger to others." He smoothed down the pleat in his smart trousers. "Well, thank you for telling me. If you'll excuse me, I have a very busy day."

I stayed put. "You mentioned justice."

He frowned again. His Botox was being put to the test today.

"You see, while Nerissa has killed two humans, someone else murdered ten school children and two teachers."

"That's terrible!"

"It is," I agreed. "And we've been up all night trying to find the culprit. You see, it turns out that the new hotel is being financed by an offshore company – Mountain Capital – very hush hush, apparently, they're involved with a lot of the regeneration in Cardiff. But what surprised me most was that they were offered a grant from the city to help finance the project."

"And? Do you want my clerk to dig out the records for that grant?" Sweat beaded on his forehead and the stale scent of fear wafted under his expensive cologne.

"Don't worry yourself about that, we found the records. And we called in some favours with an accounting firm to dig into the company. It's amazing how fast vampire accountants can work with the proper motivation. You can imagine my surprise when we found out that you are one of the beneficiaries."

Mayor Taf smiled. "I think we're done here." He made to stand.

I crossed the room with supernatural speed and placed my hand on his shoulder, forcing him back into the chair.

"I don't think we are. You see, you ordered the demolition and building work that destroyed the school."

"You're going to have trouble proving that," he said through gritted teeth.

I released him and stood back. "The contractors you employed are more than happy to make a statement in court and we have more than enough here to hand you over for embezzlement of city funds and I'm sure there's some tax evasion too." I patted the file.

He slumped down in his chair. "What do you want?"

I bent down and growled in his face. "Justice."

He looked away.

"Boss…" Maxi cautioned.

I shook my head and stepped away. "But I'll have to settle for seeing you behind bars."

His secretary sidled into the room. "I'm very sorry to interrupt sir, but there's some police officers here."

I smiled down at the mayor and crossed my arms as I watched the mundane police arrest him. It was a form of justice. Not my preferred form for a lowlife like him, but it was better than nothing. I sighed. There was still something I had to do.

~

Back on the jetty, I watched the sun sink into the sea, bathing the world in an orange caress. Beside me, I heard the water bubble up.

"Lir."

"Do you have justice for me?"

I turned to him. "The man responsible has been arrested."

"It's not enough!"

"I know." I handed over a packet.

He took it cautiously with his webbed hands. "What is this?"

"It's a protection order. Your people and your home are now officially under the protection of the Magical Liaison Office and the city requires your permission for any new buildings in any part of Cardiff Bay. I had it laminated so you could take it underwater."

Lir laughed at that and studied the seal on the official document. "Thank you, Agent Jones. Perhaps this protection of the future is something we can live with in place of justice for the past."

"What will you do with Nerissa?"

He sighed. "She is grieving. It is no excuse, but I think it merits some understanding. I have sent her to another colony so that her mind may heal."

I nodded.

"Fare well then Agent Jones. I pray we do not meet again." He placed his right hand over his heart and bowed before diving back into the sea.

I sighed and turned my back on the sea and the setting sun. "Drink?" I asked Maxi and Dot.

"Yah!"

"What do you call a group of mermaids anyway?"

"A sadness?" Dot suggested.

"A pod." Maxi replied. He always had the textbook answer.

I mussed his already messy hair and led the way to the closest bar. It wasn't enough. None of it was enough. But it was the best I could do today. And I'd have to live with that.

Wild Santa

Kidnappings. Dark elves. This Christmas is going to be wild!

When Santa gets wind of someone kidnapping children on Christmas Eve Eve, he knows he can't leave it to the authorities. Can he rescue a child, defeat dark elves intent on stealing the magic of the season and save Christmas? And how many Christmas song titles can the author crowbar into a short story?

This story was first published in the Slay Bells Ring anthology where authors were given a prompt to think about Santa as an operator. I think I did Santa justice, but I couldn't resist giving Agent Jones a cameo role.

Santa sucked slowly on the fat, stripy candy cane in his hand as if it were a fine Cuban cigar. He frowned as he read the piece of crumpled paper in his hand. This was not good. Not good at all. He sighed and bit off a chunk of the peppermint-flavoured candy. There was only one thing for it. He was going to have to clean up the Extra Naughty List.

This was not something he would have considered under normal circumstances. If he was honest with himself, he was getting on a bit, and it wasn't like the security services weren't a lot better, or at least a lot better armed, than they had been the last time he'd gotten involved. Normally, he'd leave things to them and let politicians argue over the dictators and corruption in the world. His job was simply to deliver the presents... but…this was different. Bigger than normal. And he wasn't sure he could trust the usual forces to sort it out. Plus, it involved kids, which wound him up tighter than a wind-up toy car on Christmas morning.

With a sigh, he heaved himself out of his upholstered leather chair and walked to his work wardrobe. He shunted aside the fur-trimmed uniforms for his Christmas Eve rounds, eventually finding it-stuffed at the back, neglected and well-worn. He smiled as he selected his armoured suit. It was still red, of course; he did have a reputation to uphold. But it was cunningly woven with protection charms thanks to his connections with the dwarves, who had earned themselves a little leeway with minor transgressions thanks to that favour. He struggled into the fabric. It fitted more snugly than he remembered. He adjusted himself, wincing slightly as the metal cup chafed around his intimate area. Too many mince pies, he supposed—still, nothing he could do about that now.

Suitably dressed, he moved to his armoury, glad he hadn't moved it out of his private workshop. He pulled the brass lever, and a section of the wall parted to reveal a stockpile of weapons, all arranged as neatly as the tools on his workbench. He perused the guns, grenades, and missiles as well as the more customised weapons in his arsenal. Santa grinned. It had been a long time since he'd been in the field, and he'd forgotten how much he enjoyed the preparation. He discarded the sabre he'd used to help good king Wenceslas out of a sticky jam in tenth-century Bohemia. He made his choices, placing each weapon onto the table with a sort of reverence as he remembered previous missions.

Humming a Christmas carol to himself, he pulled the lever again, and the weapons disappeared behind the hidden wall panel. The only evidence they even existed was the large pile of munitions on his wooden workbench. Now the only question was how to move them to his sleigh without attracting any attention.

He stroked his beard as he considered. It was December 23rd. The workshop would be busy, filled with North Pole elves as they made final preparations for Christmas. Survivors of a distant realm, the small, pointy-eared creatures were actually more akin to dwarves with their talent for making things and engineering. And only one thing could distract the dedicated elves from their task on Christmas Eve eve. Santa smiled and picked up his brass intercom cone.

Half an hour later, he strode out of his private workshop with a glint in his eye and announced, "Cookies for everyone in the kitchen! Take a well-earned break!"

Amidst the thanks and the excited chatter that followed the offer of baked goods, Santa grabbed a hessian sack from his office and put it gingerly into his spare sleigh. He winced as the weapons ground against each other with a metallic grating. Not the sort of noise he could easily attribute to wrapped toys. But the workshop had emptied. He grinned. He would have to make an extra special present for Mrs Claus this year to say thank you for the rush job of baking a few hundred sugar cookies.

With a pang of guilt, Santa briefly thought of his wife. Should he tell her? He shook his head, his white beard fluttering slightly in the wind as he opened the door. Best not to involve her. He took a feathered quill and dipped it into a pot of black ink before penning a quick note telling her not to worry… or to wait up.

He selected his two fastest reindeer: Dasher and Prancer. Both known for their speed at the North Pole. Lesser-known were their abilities to outmanoeuvre miscreants in a high-speed dogfight or their steadfastness in the face of mortal danger. He harnessed them quickly and gave each an appreciative tickle behind the ear. You're probably imagining some sweet cartoonish creatures with goofy grins on their muzzles. Well, you'd be wrong. Imagine instead an angry eight-foot horse, all muscle, sweat steaming in the cold air. Now add two feet of hard antlers to that horse. And more temper. Now you're close. What more could a man ask for when confronting one of the biggest villains he'd ever faced?

He hauled his bulky form into the driving seat of his spare sleigh, or as he liked to think of it: The Sleigh-er 2000. With a flick of his wrists, the reins tightened, the silver bells jingled, and Dasher and Prancer sped out of the open door into the dark sky. It was time for a sleigh ride.

Under the sparkling stars, Santa thought about his self-selected mission. It wasn't going to be easy to find and destroy a criminal organisation kidnapping children. He pulled another candy cane from his top pocket and chewed it thoughtfully, but if it were easy, it wouldn't be fun now, would it? The real question was: where to start?

Santa pulled out a scroll and unravelled it, using the flickering light attached to the cockpit of The Sleigh-er to read the magical text. His eyes travelled down until he found a familiar name. He smiled to himself. Of course. He turned his team towards the United Kingdom with a yank on the reins. He rode the aurora borealis or Northern Lights until the familiar rooftops of Cardiff hove into view. He pulled up sharply to avoid a high-rise hotel he had forgotten was there.

Would people never stop putting up fudging buildings? He shook his head and went to the one place where all supernatural miscreants gathered: The Goat.

Santa strolled through the heavy wooden door with its iron grille covering a peephole – a relic from a bygone era. He ignored the olde worlde ambiance created by the dark wooden beams and the flickering candle effect lighting. Instead, he headed straight for the bar.

"A whisky, please, Goat, and some information…"

The giant troll who owned the place started at the familiar booming voice, "Not seen you here in a while," he commented as he poured the amber liquid into a glass tumbler.

"Is Bethan around?"

Goat nodded his balding head towards the back of the pub, where a group of green-skinned kobolds were playing cards. Santa smiled his thanks and headed that way. He sank into an empty chair at Bethan's table and plonked his drink on the stained wooden surface. The kobold glared at the intruder before meeting Santa's eyes. She licked her lips.

"Well, well, Santa baby!"

Bethan's easy laugh dissolved as Santa's gaze bore into her.

"Why don't you get another round in boys?" she dismissed her cronies easily and folded her arms. "So, what brings the big man down from the North Pole two days before Christmas? You can't be here for me; I donated to charity this year…"

Santa quirked one bushy eyebrow.

"Well, I thought about giving someone some money. It's the thought that counts, right?"

"Actually, I'm not here for you." The kobold visibly sagged with relief. "I need to know about the dark elves."

Bethan leaned back, her yellow eyes filled with fear. She shook her head. "I don't know anything."

"Come on now, Bethan, you know everything that goes on in this city and plenty that happens elsewhere too. And I know that children have been going missing. Lots of children. Mundane and magical beings. Even kobolds. And I know who's behind it. So all I need from you is a location."

"Look, even if I did know something, I can't tell you. They'd kill me."

Santa stroked his beard, then waved his fingers. Strands of tinsel and light wound around the small creature, pinning her to the wooden chair. He reached down to his leather boot and pulled out a large Bowie knife. He placed it onto the table pointedly. "I can make life very uncomfortable for you. So much that you might wish they'd kill you."

Bethan panted as she tried to squirm free. Santa finished his drink and then leaned forward. "I'm going to give you until the count of three, and then I'm going to start breaking baubles. One…Two…"

"Alright, alright. All I know is that there's a warehouse in the Bay. That's where they take them. But I don't know anything more! I swear! That's all I know!" her voice squeaked up an octave as Santa leaned across the table, knife in hand.

"See, that wasn't so hard, was it?" Santa cut through the sparkly tinsel with a quick movement of the blade. "Maybe you'll even end up on the Nice List this year."

With a chuckle, Santa left the small kobold with her eyes boggling out of her green face and headed back into the night.

Dasher pawed the ground and snorted as Santa heaved himself back into The Sleigh-er. "To the Bay!" he announced before flicking the reins to signal the reindeer to take off. They might not have been able to use the Northern Lights, but the North Pole reindeer were still magical, and less than three minutes later, Santa pulled on the leather reins to slow the team as they passed the Bay. He disregarded the gentrified wine bars and restaurants that lined the waterfront, their lights gleaming on the soft waves that lapped against the concrete false harbour. Instead, he flew over the armadillo-shaped opera house with its armoured panelling glinting gently in the silent night and headed for the darker parts of Cardiff.

He swerved to avoid a small black drone camouflaged against the night sky. He frowned and took it down with a well-aimed shot to one of its rotary blades before the camera could focus on his sleigh. So many companies were copying the designs he had come up with in his workshop nowadays. It was almost criminal the amount of plagiarism he had to endure to keep his presence a secret.

He put it from his mind and took out a small brown spyglass. He sighted through the lens and studied the warehouses from the sky. It was the middle of the night, and most buildings were quiet. Except....There. Santa spotted movement.

Someone was sneaking furtively around one of the large warehouses. Santa stroked his beard, then selected his weapons. Tooled up, he leapt from the sleigh. He spread his arms, and the wings sewn into his armoured suit blew into place. With skill borne from years of experience, he dove toward the intruder.

He was almost upon them, air rushing through his beard, when he became aware that something was wrong. The figure turned and loosed a crossbow bolt directly at him. Santa swerved. The bolt bounced off his armoured suit, but he still felt the impact. That was going to leave a bruise. Santa looked up and swore. He was too close to the ground. He tried to right himself. Too late. He collided with a stack of pallets. Wood splintered. Nails ricocheted. Santa rolled himself to the side and then stopped. A crossbow bolt pointed straight at his red nose.

"Who the dzrak are you, and what the dzrak are you doing interrupting my mission?"

Santa blinked and tried to focus on the person—the woman—holding the crossbow. "You don't know who I am?"

"Rules are that the person with the crossbow pointed at your face asks the questions, Red. Start answering, or this'll be your last Christmas."

"I'm Santa Claus, and I'm here to stop a kidnapping ring."

The woman tapped her booted foot and narrowed her eyes. Santa heard the safety click off the crossbow. He swallowed hard and inched his hand slowly to the piece at his hip.

"What?" the woman barked.

"Er…" Santa started. She motioned to him to shut up, then nodded. She tapped her ear. Santa breathed a sigh of relief. She wasn't mad; she was just talking to someone on the other end of an earpiece. "Seems your story checks out. I suppose you took out our eyes in the sky, and that's your reindeer team hovering in our no-fly zone?"

Santa nodded. That explained the drone. The woman lowered her weapon and offered Santa her hand. She pulled him up easily. "Agent Jones. Magical Liaison Office, Cardiff branch. Now stay out of my way."

The woman marched off around the other side of the warehouse.

"Just a minute!" Santa hissed. Then he stopped. Agent Jones sprinted back around the building, pursued by four lanky figures with side arms. She was fast, but they were outpacing her. Dark elves. Santa drew his twin guns holstered on either side of his broad hips, Holly and Ivy, and opened fire.

Agent Jones slipped behind the cover of the broken pallets and let off a crossbow bolt. Two dark elves were down—two more to go. Santa dived over the pallets, wriggling as his stomach snagged on a sharp piece of wood. With a grunt, he yanked himself free and fell to the ground. He risked a peek through the shattered woodpile. The dark elves held off, re-loading their weapons.

"Come out, and we'll let you live," one of them tried. He couldn't quite keep the snigger from his voice.

"Think you can cover me?" Agent Jones asked.

Santa checked his ammo and nodded. Without another word, the agent leapt forward, shifting into a large cat mid-air. Santa's twinkling eyes widened with shock before he ducked to the side and unloaded one of his clips into the farthest dark elf. The creature staggered back from the impact and sank to the ground. Emboldened, Santa stepped from his cover to help Agent Jones. He stopped when he saw the heavy lynx clawing the lifeless body of the remaining elf.

"Good kitty," he couldn't help himself.

The shifter morphed back into her human form and pushed him up against the cold wall of the warehouse. "Say that again!"

Santa squeaked out an apology. He weighed…well; he didn't like to admit exactly how many pounds of heavy muscle covered with a generous portion of shock-absorbing fat he weighed—but it was a lot. And this woman had him pinned by the throat as if he were a delicate slip of a thing. Having made her point, she dropped him. Santa wheezed as he caught his breath, but refused to sink to the ground. She tilted her head, listening to something.

"I can hear a child," Agent Jones assessed the warehouse, looking for a covert entrance. "I don't suppose you can get us in, can you?"

Santa pulled on his beard and closed his eyes for a moment. Then he smiled, "Actually, I can." He grabbed her hand and tapped the side of his nose. A split second later, the pair were inside the building underneath a Christmas tree. Real pine.

The effect was somewhat spoiled by the half-hearted attempt to dress its branches with plastic baubles. Something was off.

Santa turned. "Oh, fudge sticks."

More dark elves surrounded them. And they were all packing heat.

"At last, here comes Santa Claus! Welcome, welcome, Mr Claus. I must say, I was expecting you months ago, but better late than never. And almost perfect timing! It's Christmas Eve Eve!" the dark elf laughed. It was a clipped sort of sound that must have made the rest of the elves feel nervous because they all joined in laughing humourlessly too.

Santa looked around, trying to estimate whether he had enough firepower to blast his way out. Agent Jones looked like she was making the same calculations. But there was still the child to account for.

"Are you looking for the little girl?" the dark elf held up a phone and clicked a button. A young voice rang out, "Please, help me! Please!"

He laughed again, "The great Santa Claus cannot even tell the difference between a real child and a recording!"

"I can tell you what you'll get for Christmas; you sack of sh…"

"Ah, ah-ah, naughty, naughty, Mr Claus," the dark elf waggled one long finger at Santa, "There's no need for language. Not when all I want from you is something so easy for you to give me—but where are my manners? Who is this? A friend of yours?"

"Agent Jones, Magical Liaison Office, and you're all under arrest for kidnapping, child trafficking, and smuggling magical items. Now hand yourselves in, and I won't add resisting arrest to those charges."

"Oho! Very funny! Tie her up. Santa and I need to talk."

Agent Jones twisted away from the dark elf, who had to win the 'most stupid' award for moving forward to tie up the shifter. She landed a punch that sent him flying. Before she could take out any more of the grey-skinned figures, one of them cracked her on the back of the head with the butt of an assault rifle. She fell to the ground. Unconscious. They proceeded to tie her up and then stepped back, guns trained on Santa. One of them frisked him and grunted as they took his assault rifle, pistols, and grenades from their holsters and laid them on a bench.

"Now that that unpleasantness is out of the way, all I want is the magic of Christmas…"

"What?!"

"Yes, the magic of Christmas. I need something powerful enough to get me to my true home, you see," the dark elf's face turned wistful, and he looked off to the East as if he could see whichever cursed fae realm he had sprung from. "So tell me, Santa, will you take me to the source?"

Santa tried not to laugh, "There is no source. The magic of Christmas springs from the belief in people's hearts, children especially."

The dark elf sighed, "That's what I thought you might say." He snapped his long fingers, and another lanky figure appeared, hustling a small child in front of them.

"The hearts of children, hmmm?" the elf drew a cruel, serrated blade from his belt and twisted it around in his elegant hand. He moved towards the child. The young girl's head flopped to the side. At least she was unconscious. Santa moved forward. Dark elves blocked his path, guns resting on his broad chest. The knife moved closer to the child's chest. Santa watched in horror. Surely no one would be that cruel. But the blade kept going.

Less than a centimetre away from the girl's panda pyjama top, Santa couldn't take it anymore. "Stop!"

The dark elf smiled and holstered the knife back to his belt with a flourish. "You see, that wasn't so difficult, was it? Now, you will take me to the source of your power at the North Pole. And to ensure there isn't any funny business, we will take young Ciara with us. Now call down the friendly beasts."

Santa nodded dumbly. He couldn't think of anything else to do. He was outnumbered, outgunned, and outmanoeuvred. He allowed himself to be led outside. He looked up to the patch of sky where he knew his faithful reindeer team would be waiting. In the distance, he heard church bells toll twelve slow strikes. Christmas Eve.

"Get on with it!" A gun barrel jabbed against his back. Santa let out a loud whistle. A twinkle in the sky became brighter as the sleigh careened towards the ground. Santa considered pushing the leader in front of the speeding sleigh—but he was carrying the small girl. He couldn't risk it.

Dasher and Prancer pulled up at the last moment and landed the sleigh with the practised ease of animals born to it. Or at least had logged thousands of hours at the North Pole flight simulator. Santa climbed in. He had until they got to the North Pole to think of something. If he didn't—well, it didn't bear thinking about. The dark elves would destroy the workshop in their anger when they discovered there was no magic source. Santa had no doubt his elves would put up a good fight; he'd drilled them in defensive manoeuvres himself. But they'd have no warning. Unless…

Santa leaned forward as the leader pulled himself up along with the child. Unfortunately, there was ample room in the back of the sleigh for over twenty of the magical miscreants, and they quickly piled in. Santa held his breath and allowed his hand to brush the control panel as he picked up the reins. With a half-hearted "Yah," the reindeer lifted off the ground.

Santa deliberately didn't try to find any aurora strands to ride, but his animals still ate up the sky as swiftly as a jet as they followed the star to the East and then tilted Northwards. Santa could only hope his distress call had been heeded.

"You made the right choice," called the dark elf next to him as he stroked the girl's soft black hair.

Santa considered pulling his team into a loop-the-loop as they careened across the North Sea, but the sleeping form of Ciara stopped him. Instead, he allowed his reindeer to drift into the light turbulence of some low-hanging clouds and took grim satisfaction in one of the elves throwing up. By the angry noises behind him, it sounded like the dark elf hadn't quite made it to the edge of the sleigh.

And still, the sleigh sped closer to the North Pole winter wonderland. To his home.

Santa landed the sleigh hard, and, to their credit, the reindeer didn't protest as they pounded the icy runway just south of his workshop. The open flats of the North Pole were eerily quiet. Too quiet. Then Santa saw a familiar solitary figure approaching; a thick recurve bow slung across their back.

Even with her furs on, Mrs Claus' distinctive curves were visible. She had been a Valkyrie before marrying Santa and hadn't lost her looks or keen battle skills. The dark elves jumped down from the sleigh, shivering in the arctic winds as they aimed their weapons at the tall, blonde woman. Santa glanced at the sleeping Ciara. He had to get her inside before she froze.

"You left without your scarf. I don't know how many times I have to tell you!" Mrs Claus handed him a festive scarf emblazoned with Christmas trees.

The dark elves relaxed, taking Mrs Claus for a bustling, busybody wife. Santa tried not to smile. Instead, he tried to gesture with his eyes at the small child.

"You're right as always, dear. These are some… ah… friends who wanted to see the workshop." Santa hoped she picked up on his code.

Mrs Claus nodded brightly and clapped her hands together, "Of course, well, you must come in and warm yourselves.

There's hot cocoa and cookies, made with my special blend of Christmas spices."

Santa hoped she was just acting as Mrs Claus led the way to the workshop. She opened a door and let the weary band of dark elves into the workshop. It was eerily quiet. The door clicked shut in the silence, and Santa heard the heavy key turn in the lock. He tried to catch his wife's eye. The workshop was normally bustling with the North Pole elves. Now the benches were full of toys, but where the fudge was everyone?

The leader of the dark elves handed the child to one of his minions before taking out his long serrated knife and aiming it at Mrs Claus' throat. The Valkyrie blinked her icy blue eyes as the dark elf spoke, "We're here for the magic of Christmas, so don't try anything stupid."

The tallest of the dark elves had moved towards an abandoned workbench and picked up a tiny toy gun, no bigger than a robin redbreast. Santa narrowed his eyes. The dark elf looked down the barrel. Santa turned away and edged towards the elf holding the girl. The tall elf pressed the trigger. His head exploded. Santa felt the chunks of gore land in his white beard.

"What the?" the elves pointed guns at each other in confusion. Santa dived forward, covering the child and the elf with his bulk. A string of gunfire hammered into the insulated wooden ceiling. Santa brought his elbow down on the elf's nose and wrestled the child from his thin hands. Then, cradling the girl, he scooted under the nearest bench.

More gunshots rebounded around the huge workspace. It was hard for Santa to see what happened next in the confusion. Wrapped presents exploded in bursts of fire, sending wrapping paper and toy shrapnel flying. His wife whirled and elbowed the leader in his sharp nose before ducking for cover next to Santa. Then, with an easy push, she tipped the bench over so it was sheltering them.

"You're an angel; I could kiss you!"

"Wait until we're underneath the missile toe," she smiled at him as she chucked a green and white plant sprig into the air. The plump berries detached themselves from the leaves and rained down in streaks of fire. They stuck to the dark elves before exploding. In the fiery glow, Mrs Claus leaned forward and kissed her husband. "Ugh, is that someone's blood?"

"Er…" Santa mumbled something non-committal. Mrs Claus might have been a retired Valkyrie, but she had never actually feasted on the bodies of her enemies. "We need to get the child to safety."

Mrs Claus nodded and unslung her bow.

"You brought a bow to a gunfight?"

The Valkyrie shrugged one mighty shoulder and shot Santa a saucy wink, "There's always time for a bow at Christmas!" With that, she nocked one of her personal arrows, the ones with flights made from arctic eagle feathers, and aimed.

The squelch of flesh told Santa that his wife's aim had been true. Naturally. As his wife covered him, Santa crawled along the length of the bench. His fingers itched to join the fight, but he had to keep the girl safe and get some weapons after the dark elves had left his munitions in the warehouse. He searched around for an escape route. The door to his office was on the other side of the workshop; nothing except weapons were there. His eyes darted around the wooden walls of the workshop and stopped. There. Gesturing frantically with dextrous fingers, he recognised the wide eyes of Merry Bobbins, one of his senior North Pole elves, peeking from a vent.

Using his body as a shield, Santa broke cover and fled towards the vent, gripping the child tightly in his arms. Bullets hit his armoured suit, each one a painful impact on his body despite his protective clothing. He dived the last few feet and curled his body around the small girl.

"Take her!" he shouted at Merry. The elderly elf took the sleeping child and pulled her quickly into the vent.

"Any other civilians?" she asked.

Santa shook his head.

"You'd better watch out..."Merry grinned and gave a long whistle to the tune of Deck the Halls. Less than three seconds later, the frosted skylight opened and Santa's elves rappelled down ropes fashioned from fairy lights. They streamed into the workshop, tossing flash-bang grenades at the intruders. Santa hadn't included this in his defensive training!

He stuck to the sides of the workshop, watching in awe as Ginger Jingles fired a converted Nerf gun at two of the elves. The dark elves responded with bolts of magic as well as gunfire. Santa edged his way to his private workshop and let himself in just as a pile of toys exploded under a barrage of Christmas fireworks from Tinsel McTinselface.

Inside his workshop, Santa took a deep breath and pulled the brass lever for the second time that day. His favourite weapons had gone, left at the warehouse. But he had been stockpiling for centuries. He quickly holstered a long, bone-handled knife in his leather belt and grabbed a pair of antique pistols. A gold barrel caught his eye. The Peacemaker. He ran his fingers over the pistol. He'd modified it from a standard magnum with extra barrels and custom bullets. It only gave him one shot. But that was all he needed. He loaded the chamber quickly and headed back into the fray.

Ducking under the spray from a blunderbuss gun that seemed to be firing hard-boiled humbugs, Santa aimed. Pulling the Peace-maker's trigger, Santa unleashed six 44mm exploding bullets at a dark elf who had risked putting their head above an overturned workbench. Her grey face disappeared in a cloud of red mist.

"Ho Ho Ho Motherfudgers!" Santa exclaimed. He dropped the spent Peacemaker and smoothly pulled the antique pistols from his belt. The polished walnut stocks were slightly thicker than you might expect—a testament to the expert engineer's modifications to convert the guns into semi-automatic weapons. Then, with a practised motion, Santa dived for cover, letting loose a barrage of bullets. He landed on his side next to Mrs Claus, who was chucking bauble grenades across the workshop as if she did it every day.

"How many left?" Santa asked, replacing the clips in his semi-automatic pistols.

Mrs Claus turned to look at her husband. Her fur cap had fallen to the ground, letting her long blonde hair flow freely around her face. Fudge, but she was kissable. He realised she'd said something. "What?"

"Still a dozen to go, but they're low on bullets, and we're just getting started." Mrs Claus's eyes flashed with excitement.

Santa nodded and heaved himself up, guns blazing. Mrs Claus joined his fire with her own arrows. Just like the old days. He mowed down two more elves before his ears registered the quiet. He turned. And stopped. The dark elf leader had Mrs Claus.

He pinned her with one arm while the other held his curved blade across her throat. "I think that's enough, don't you? Weapons down! Now!"

Santa put his guns down on the ground with exaggerated slowness. He motioned to the North Pole elves to do the same. The noise of weapons meeting the worn wooden floor reverberated around the workshop. A sproing pulled Santa's attention. Tinsel McTinselface shrugged apologetically as one of his homemade contraptions unravelled in a cacophony of pings and clicks.

"Good. Now you will take us to the source of your power, or I will cut this woman's throat like a pig."

The North Pole elves gasped. Partly in shock. Partly in disbelief. There was no source of Christmas magic. You might as well try to bottle hope or fear. Pairs of large unblinking eyes looked to Santa for an answer. Santa sighed heavily, feeling every one of his thousands of years old. How had it come to this? He was going to lose his wife and probably his workshop over a fairy tale.

"I keep it in my private office," he managed. At least that bought him some time.

"Lead the way, fat man!"

Santa moved slowly. It felt as though someone had replaced his boots with lead. His hands fell to his sides. And touched his knife. The hard bone handle was reassuring somehow. It was an ancient knife. A weapon he hadn't touched since—since he couldn't remember when. He felt something else rising through his blood. Something he hadn't felt in aeons. Something he hadn't felt since… before. Since before he had been turned into this old, fat sack of pudding. Since before he had settled permanently here in the North Pole. Since before he had provided shelter for the outcast elves with their dwarven heritage. He felt the feeling well up inside him. Power. Steel. Chaos. Wind began to move his beard. Softly at first, then stronger, stronger.

"What's going on?" the dark elf interrupted Santa's introspection.

Santa turned and drew his blade. His normally twinkly eyes glinted with something dangerous. The dark elf took a step back.

"You are in my realm, fae." Santa's voice held undercurrents of thunder. His suit no longer seemed the bright, cheery red of commercials and instead matched the spilled blood on the floor.

The dark elf's eyes widened in fear.

"Oh," breathed Mrs Claus, and the Valkyrie actually blushed, "you sound like when we met at the first noel."

"Quiet!" snarled the dark elf.

"Release her!" A crash accompanied Santa's words as his eight reindeer burst through the workshop doors. With rumbling snorts, they made their way to their master. The dark elves shouted as they were pushed aside. One lifted a gun at Vixen, who immediately speared him through the chest with sharp antlers. Vixen shook her huge head. The body slumped to the floor. Bloodied, she took her place in the herd around Santa.

The dark elf looked on in bewildered terror. This was not the jolly fat man of Christmas commercials and holiday cheer. This was something darker. Something ancient.

The dark elf swallowed. "What is this?"

"Release her now," Santa reached down into the depths of his other powers and found a name, "Mordred."

The dark elf swallowed; his skin took on a paler pallor. His black eyes darted around the room, taking in his nervous comrades, surrounded by ginormous reindeer, taking in the wide watching eyes of the North Pole elves that seemed tinged with a wildness he hadn't noticed before. He looked back to Santa. Gone was the old, fat man. Instead, there was something else there. Something ancient and powerful. Santa stood a little straighter. His bulk was now hardened muscle instead of flabby blubber. And worse. The dark elf felt the compulsion wash over him. What was this strange magic? He wanted to join the man in red. He tried to follow him. It would be an honour to be invited to join his band and hunt. Mordred shook his head, his grip on his blade loosening.

Mrs Claus felt the change in his grip and twisted herself free. She paused to deliver an elbow into Mordred's stomach before joining her spouse. Santa reached for his wife and pulled her into a warm embrace. She melted at his hard kiss, just like old times. Like the times before, he was Santa Claus, when he had been the spirit of cheer and chaos that embodied the dark of midwinter. The spirit that allowed humans and fae alike to hope in the darkest of times and bring goodwill to each other to ease the winter's passage. This spirit could just as easily dispense ill-tidings as well as glad, or bad luck as well as good. It had taken blood sacrifices as people prayed for protection and survival in the times before. This spirit had led the Wild Hunt.

Mordred flung himself forward, fighting the compulsion spilling over him. Spittle foamed at his mouth as he lunged for Santa, still not realising who he faced. The Wild Hunt leader could banish fae as well as include them. Santa lifted his hand and pointed his knife towards Mordred. The dark elf stopped in his tracks, compelled by a power he didn't comprehend.

"Mordred Pendragon, I banish you back to your cursed realm and forbid you from joining the Hunt until you come to peace with the consequences of your actions."

The dark elf's eyes widened further. "No," he started. But the knife was already glowing with old magick. Swirling tendrils of white light poured from the blade and twined themselves around the elf.

Mordred's eyes narrowed into hate-filled slits, and he spat at Santa, "I will find my way back and take what is mine by rights!"

Santa didn't even deign to reply as the dark elf shimmered and disappeared back to his own evil realm. Instead, he took a deep breath, revelling in his strength and power. Why had he let this part of him fall to one side? He snaked an arm around Mrs Claus and pulled her towards him, his lips claiming hers with primal lust.

"Er, Santa?"

Santa broke off the kiss and stared at the small elf who had interrupted him, "What should we do with them?"

Santa smiled. It was a touch ominous. In the flickering firelight of the workshop, the shape of horns could be made out above his head. He turned his head, and the illusion vanished. The wild power hadn't left him yet. "It's time to go hunting."

The North Pole elves nervously led the large reindeer out to the sleigh as Santa tied the remaining dark elves tightly with fairy lights. He chucked them into a large hessian sack that didn't seem to expand as he dumped in elf after elf, followed by the corpses of their fallen comrades.

He lifted his arms to the sky and called down the power of the Wild Hunt. A tornado swirled around him, sending the signal into the air. Flashes of light blinked on the snow as the fae folk and their beasts answered the call. From all dimensions, they came to participate in the centuries-old tradition of mayhem. Mrs Claus appeared at his side, garbed in her battle gear of gleaming breastplate and leather trousers. She carried the small girl gently, wrapped in furs and a hand-knitted scarf. Santa climbed into his sleigh, put his arm around Mrs Claus, and flicked the reins. The Hunt began.

It was a turbulent ride on the winds of chaos. Hell hounds and wish hounds bayed behind them while fae cheered and whooped. It had been a long time since the Hunt had been called. Santa drove them on, riding the aurora towards his destination. A warehouse in Cardiff. He paused the Hunt briefly to deposit the dark elves. He smiled as he adjusted the large ribbon and card he left with them for the unconscious shifter:

~

Dear Agent Jones, Merry Christmas! Thought you might enjoy this gift, love Santa x

~

He climbed back into his sleigh and made one more stop to return the sleeping Ciara home. Then they were off. The Wild Hunt rode the winds across Europe in a blur of chaos and hoofbeats that would last all night and be reported as the '*wild*

Christmas storms' and *'Midwinter Mayhem'* in papers across the continent. Santa revelled in it. In his power to bring the fae realms together for this orgy of raw, primal energy. Santa leaned over and kissed Mrs Claus passionately. It looked like it was going to be a wonderful Christmastime after all.

Spa Day

You must relax! When Agent Jones is forced to relax at an AI Spa, things go from awkward to awful. As tensions rise, can she stop a robot uprising and finally unwind?

This short story was inspired by a writing prompt 'technology vs humankind' where I started to think about how Agent Jones would react to AI and what context she would hate it in the most, and that's when it hit me that she'd hate to be forced to relax.

I narrowed my eyes. The scent of smoke curled in my nostrils. An ambush. And there was no escape. They were at my desk.

Maxi held out a cake, and they broke into an off-key rendition of the dzraking Happy Birthday song. I stared and let the candle sputter out.

I'd known something was off. Secret smiles and nods, overzealous attention to computer screens. Maxi's stupid cover story; no one volunteered to travel from London to install a software update.

"Happy Birthday, boss! You've been working so hard lately…" I could feel the charm dripping off Dot's words. Good job vampire hypnosis didn't work on me.

I grunted. I always worked hard. This wasn't news.

"So, we all clubbed together and got you a spa day," Aloora chimed in, a smile beaming on her petite face as she produced a red envelope from behind her back.

I froze. A spa day? What the dzrak? I opened my mouth, but Maxi interrupted.

"I know you don't exactly like people, so I found this new spa, very modern and operated by robots. So, you won't have to interact with anyone, yah, and it uses artificial intelligence to match the best treatments…"

He trailed off as I pursed my lips. An AI spa sounded like a nightmare – hadn't they heard of the Terminator films? I closed my mouth, then opened it again. This was a disaster. I looked up at their expectant faces. "That's a nice gesture." Three smiles broadened. There, that would do. I hadn't damaged team morale and I would rip up the gift card as soon as I got home.

"Great! It's booked for today, what, so you'd better hurry over there. Chop chop."

"Today? So sorry." I forced my mouth down into an approximation of disappointment. "I can't go today; there's too much paperwork."

Maxi raised one bushy eyebrow at the empty in-tray on my desk. I bent my head back to the computer screen and furiously clicked open some reports. "That warlock's got himself stuck in a disappearing wardrobe again."

"Not possible. We impounded that armoire last week. Trust us, boss, we can take care of everything here. It's only one afternoon away from the office. What could happen?"

"I don't think Vass would appreciate me swanning off for a spa day during work hours."

Dot laughed. "Not to worry, we checked with him first and he thought it was a great idea."

Traitor. If I couldn't rely on my grumpy department head to kibosh stupid schemes like this, what was the point of checking in with him? My thoughts turned to petty revenge; I could flood his inbox with useless reports, or maybe I could engineer a meeting with him and the city's Supernatural Board. A small smile played over my lips as I imagined Vass attending one of the long-winded sessions.

"So, you'll go, yah?" Maxi blinked at me, his face a picture of innocence.

"Sure," I forced a grin as I grabbed my jacket. They didn't know that I planned to head home instead and have my own relaxing afternoon brushing up on fighting drills.

"Great, I'll drive." Aloora spun a keyring around her fingers. Was that a smirk on the gnome's face? "I've got to head out and get some new dragon recordings."

I pursed my lips, unable to think of a way out. Desperate, I refreshed my emails. Surely there must be some emergency that needed my presence. Maybe a werewolf attack or a magical artefact gone wrong. I'd even take a dragon attack, but they'd been quiet since making their nest in the Millennium Stadium.

Nothing. Not even a complaint from a mundane non-magic user that they'd been tricked into doing something on a night out. What was the world coming to when you couldn't even rely on the mundanes to file a complaint?

"Let's go. But I'm driving."

My team waved as I stalked out of the room and led the way to our underground garage where the van waited. Aloora followed, her footsteps light on the tiled floor. I was so preoccupied that she made it to the driving seat before me.

"I said, I'm driving."

The gnome's face fell, but I was adamant. I was going to be in control of one thing on my birthday, and besides, her driving was…well, let's just say it was extreme. And I didn't want the rally experience as well as a dzraking massage session. I followed her directions and pulled up in front of a shiny, white building with enormous glass windows and a metal sign that confirmed it was a spa.

"OK, see you tomorrow." I got out of the car, intending to walk in, wait for Aloora to leave, then walk straight back out again, but the petite gnome followed me.

"I've got the voucher, and I want to make sure you get the works."

"Don't you have some research to do?"

She returned my glare with a bright smile. "Yep, I'll get straight to it after you're signed in. The dragons aren't going anywhere."

I followed her in, Dwarfish curse words ringing through my head. What was the world coming to when my team didn't trust me to go for a spa day? Perhaps I should be happy I'd hired such perceptive and persistent people…but not when their tenacity was aimed at me. Aloora skipped through the front doors, and I huffed out a sigh as we arrived at the sleek reception desk.

An android stared blankly at us; its fake human face eerily symmetrical. "Welcome to the world's first AI spa, or SpAI, as we call it. Ha. Ha. Technology helps us to match the best treatments to each client for an individual experience that guarantees relaxation. Our unique AI system links to the entire spa so we can ensure a relaxing experience. How may I help you today?"

"One full spa afternoon, please," Aloora said, slapping the envelope down on the desk.

"Absolutely. That includes our full body massage, a deep flotation experience, and we guarantee you will leave feeling relaxed. Please place your credit card in the payment machine or place a pre-paid voucher in the scanner."

Aloora slipped the voucher into the scanner while I eyed the exit.

"Please hand in your phone and any valuables and I will store them for you."

Aloora smiled at me, and I clenched my jaw as I pulled my phone out. I checked it. Come on, please let there be an emergency. Nothing.

"Best to hand over your handbag, boss."

I turned up the wattage on my glare but placed my bag onto the tray. It gave a satisfying clunk as the crossbow and knives I carried rearranged themselves. The robot passed me a key card in exchange and told me to wear it around my neck.

"Stand still and I will complete your body scan."

"What?"

"Scan completed. High degrees of tension and stress hormones found. Would you like a glass of mineral water?"

I eyed the large, clear jug on the countertop and shook my head.

"Do you have any questions before your treatment begins? I can answer anything in any style you choose, thanks to advanced chat AI."

"Really? Tell me a joke in Victoria Beckham's voice?"

The robot's artificial eyes blinked at me as Aloora rolled hers. No doubt she would have asked it something about dragons and then corrected the answer. "Two oranges walk into a bar. One says 'ouch'. The other screams 'Aaaa, a talking orange.'"

"Huh." Not a good joke, but better than small talk with human servers. Maybe there was something to the AI business after all.

"Now, please follow my fellow Spandroids and you can begin your treatment. I guarantee you will relax."

Two robots appeared from a back room, wheeled their way across the spotless floor and placed themselves on either side of me. Unlike the receptionist, these were more obviously robots in white and black, with metal glinting at their joints and a small camera built into the white casing of their cuboid heads. Blue pixels formed into semi-circles for the eyes and more pixels appeared in a mouth shape as they spoke.

"Please, follow us to relaxation."

One of them gestured with a circular palm. With a roll of my eyes, I fell in line. I just had to keep this up until Aloora headed off. I waited until she was outside, then made my move. But the dzraking robots blocked my path.

No matter, I'd let them lead me to the treatment room, then ditch this place. The robots escorted me to a changing room, and the door swung open. Not creepy at all.

I went in and the door locked behind me. Was this place a spa or a prison? I took in the light-coloured wood and inhaled the fresh pine scent as I glared at the white fluffy robe and matching white swimming costume next to it. If it was a prison, it was a lot nicer than the containment cells we used at the Magical Liaison Office.

Two other doors opened out from the changing area. Both were locked. An artificial female voice instructed me to change and asked me to select my first treatment from the menu on the screen. At least there was none of that stupid 'get to know you' rubbish I'd had to endure the last time I'd gone to a spa. I'd only wanted a sports massage, why did I need to choose a scent that defined my personality?

I stared down at the options: deep flotation, full body massage or use of the swimming pool. With a shrug, I selected the last option. At least I could get a workout in. The disembodied computer voice asked me to choose the next treatment, and I picked one at random. The fake woman thanked me for my selection and told me to exit through door one to get to the pool when I was ready. I changed and headed for the pool. The sharp stench of chlorine almost overwhelmed my sensitive nose when I stepped through.

An older lady sat in one of the cream, wicker loungers, drinking a concoction that looked like baby food. She gazed at me with a panicked look and pulled her robe around her, but I ignored her and stood at the edge of the pool. It took only a moment for me to force down the animal dislike of water from my lynx half and I dived into the warm water. Half an hour later, I decided I'd had enough front crawl and got out. I stretched, enjoying the burn in my muscles from the workout. The lady hadn't moved from her spot, but as I approached the stack of towels next to her, she grabbed my hand.

"Keep your body loose and your heartbeat low."

"What?"

She opened her mouth, but a robot on wheels zoomed into the pool area. "It is time for another juice drink. You are not yet relaxed." It handed a glass filled with something green to the lady and she took it with hands that trembled so much she spilled some of the healthy juice onto the floor.

"Miss Jones, it is time for your deep flotation treatment. Would you like a refreshment first?"

I eyed the glass. If refreshment meant blended vegetables, that was a hard pass from me. "No and I've changed my mind about the treatments. I'll go."

"You must relax."

"Don't fight them," the lady whispered from behind her drink.

I frowned as the machine handed me a robe and led me to my first treatment. It paused by a large white arch that looked like an airport security scanner.

"Please, step inside."

"For what?"

"Please, step inside."

I huffed and obeyed, rolling my eyes at the dumb machine. Jets of hot air blasted me from all sides, making my pulse race before they vanished. I was completely dry. I raised a hand to my usually sleek bob. It had puffed out into a ball of frizz around my face. I let out a growl of annoyance.

"Please follow me to your perfect deep flotation treatment."

The robot led me to another door. This one opened onto a dark corridor with tiny lights embedded in the ceiling, probably to mimic the stars or some other spiritual nonsense. "Please enter flotation room one and get into the tank to begin your relaxation experience."

"Look, I don't need–"

"Your heartbeat is elevated and your body is showing signs of stress. Please enter flotation room one to begin your relaxation experience." It moved to block the exit back to the swimming pool and, with a sigh, I decided it would be easier to follow the path of least resistance and get into the dzraking flotation device.

Inside the room was a large pod filled with water and lit by faint blue lights. Lavender wafted through a vent and made me sneeze. The robot waited by the door and, with another sigh, I took off my robe and got into the pod. The lid closed.

"Wait. What the dzrak?" I tried to get out, but it was too late. I was trapped. With no other choice, I lay in the warm water. What was I meant to do now? I tapped my foot against the end of the tank. Was I just meant to stay in here? Panpipe music surrounded me. Dzrak no. I winced as my sensitive ears reacted to the song. Give me nineties pop any day of the week, but this…nope.

I knocked on the lid. "I'm ready to get out now."

"You will get out when you are relaxed."

I frowned. What was a robot going to do about it? I pushed on the lid. Locked. My heart rate spiked, and I pounded on the top of the tank.

"You must relax."

"Like dzrak am I relaxing in this water coffin." I braced my feet on the floor and angled myself to push against the lid, using my shifter strength. The lid cracked open as the locking mechanism burst under my brute force.

"You must relax." The sliver of an opening closed as the robot used its clamp-like hands to press the tank together, its pixelated eyes staring at me through the gap.

Dzrak this. No robot keeps me in a box. I shifted my angle and braced again. This time, the lid didn't budge. I punched the lid in frustration. The box rocked under the force of my blow. A smile curved my lips. I squatted in the body temperature water and rocked my body from side to side, building momentum as the flotation tank shifted with me. I ignored the nausea building in my stomach as the water swirled around me.

"Breach of protocol one zero one. You must complete your treatment."

I ignored the robotic voice and kept up my rocking motion until the tank tumbled from its pedestal, flying open and spilling water and me out onto the floor. I slid over the tiles and hit the wall hard. But I was free. I couldn't help the grin that spread over my face as I saw the tank had landed on the robot. I grabbed my robe and headed for the door, the strobed red light of a silent alarm reflecting off the huge puddle spreading across the room.

Five robots zoomed towards me. "Miss Jones, you are not relaxed."

"What are you talking about? This is the best I've felt all day."

"Ha. Ha. It is time for your massage."

"I don't want a dzraking massage."

"Ha. Ha. Come with us."

Two robots gripped my arms with inhuman strength and led me back towards the swimming pool, the stench of chlorine and essential oils making me sneeze. Maybe it was better to play along for now. The others set about cleaning up the mess in the flotation room.

I shot the old lady a look as the machines hustled me past. Her worried eyes grew large. What was her deal?

The machines changed direction and led me to another corridor. This one was underlit with a soft warm white light, probably meant to represent candles or inner peace or something. They stopped outside treatment room two and the door slid open with a quiet click.

They pushed me into the room and I whirled round in time to see the door slide shut. I pressed my fingertips to the doorframe, scrabbling to prise the door open, but I couldn't get a grip on the smooth wood.

I narrowed my eyes and contemplated the room. No windows. It was dark. A prickle of light appeared as one of the artificial candles on a shelf turned on. As I watched, the remaining candles flickered on one by one. Like a horror movie. A padded table dominated the room. It had a hole cut out of one end.

"Miss Jones, please remove your robe and lie on the table so your deep relaxation massage can begin."

I folded my arms.

"Miss Jones, your scan showed extreme tension in your shoulders and neck. We tailor each massage to the individual and will help you unwind."

"I doubt that."

"Your treatment is ready to begin. Please remove your robe and lie on the table."

With no other options, I complied and lay face down on the table, my body tensed. "Just get this over with so I can go home."

A whirring noise made my head spin round and mechanical tentacles lowered from the ceiling, different attachments glowing in the candlelight as they reached for my skin. I pushed myself up, but they were fast, colliding with my back and legs, forcing me back onto the table. Wasn't there some rule about robots not hurting people? As I strained against the machine, something that felt like three ball bearings inside a flannel rubbed over my shoulders.

"How is the pressure?"

"It's a little hard," I said through gritted teeth.

The pressure eased but was still enough to keep me pressed against the table. The snakelike arms kneading my back, pummelling my skin as they ran over every inch of me, digging into each knot of tension they found.

I counted seconds in my head until I reached three hundred then I spoke. "I think that's enough."

"You are still experiencing stress and tension. The treatment will continue."

"For how long?"

"Until you are relaxed."

And something clicked in my head. How long had the old woman been here for? The robots wouldn't let clients go until they relaxed. My shoulders tensed at the realisation and the pressure pads rotated faster over my muscles, pinning me to the bench but doing nothing to get rid of the knots in my muscles. I had to get out of here and shut this AI down.

"I think my hand is feeling tense."

Immediately, the tentacles moved down my arms to massage my palms. A smile curved my lips. I grabbed the end of the snaking arm and held on tight.

"You must release the massage unit so we can complete your treatment."

I clenched my fist, keeping hold as the machine tried to pull away. The other tentacles stopped as the robot dealt with my breach in protocol. That was the opening I needed. I twisted, keeping my grip tight, and yanked down the snaking arm. It disconnected from the ceiling with a fizz of wires.

The remaining arms shrank back, and I saw a blue light in the centre. The AI. I gave it the finger and walked to the door. A rush of air pressed against my back. I ducked and rolled to avoid an arm as it reached for me. As it snaked towards me again, I raised one eyebrow and tensed up. I jumped and ran up it, using my catlike agility to keep my balance. Another tentacle made a grab for me. I dodged it and leapt, gripping its casing as it flailed.

I dismounted with a forward flip and weaved past thrusting arms, arcing in a circle around it. I mixed it up every so often by rolling through the centre and jumping over and through the writhing mechanical mass. It was almost fun. The best workout I'd had in years. I cricked my neck and executed a perfect backflip.

The tentacles reached for me and stopped. I could hear the straining wires beneath the casing. I patted the nearest one, all tied up with its other tentacles. Stupid machines. I smirked and climbed up the knotted arms until I could look the stupid AI straight in its robotic eye.

"No one forces me to unwind."

I punched its light out. Literally. My fist crunched into the eye with an explosion of black glass and the tentacles went limp. I picked the glass from my hand and let it fall to the floor with a satisfying ping before jumping down.

The door burst open. Four robots wheeled into the room, blue eyes staring as they scanned the destruction.

"This is not relaxed." The leader stretched its hands towards me. But I'd had enough. I leapt at the robot and used it as a springboard to clear the others, landing in the corridor with a crouch. I sprinted towards the closing door and skidded through as it slid shut.

The old lady stared at me, a drink in hand.

"Come on, I'm busting us out of here."

"Thank the lord." She stood. "What's the plan?"

"Get our clothes. Grab my handbag and get the dzrak out of here."

I grabbed her hand just as the first robot whizzed through the door to the treatment rooms. The old lady flung her juice at it, landing a direct hit on its pixelated face. The green gloop dripped down, covering its camera sensor. It stopped dead. Good to know. But the others streamed after it.

I shifted my grip, hefted the lady onto my shoulders with ease, and fled.

"On your right," she called out a warning as more robots sped into the swimming pool area. I put her down on a lounger and spun, executing a perfect roundhouse that sent one flying into the water. It sparked and went silent. The others kept coming. I couldn't fight them all like this, not with a civilian in the room.

"I'll distract them. You get out of here."

"How are you going to distract them?"

"Just run."

I paused on the edge of the pool and shifted into my large lynx form. Weren't expecting that, were you, robots? Red light reflected from the pool as the silent alarm kicked in.

"No animals in the spa."

I bared my teeth at the robots as they crowded me. The old lady boggled for less than a second before she legged it. At least she wasn't one of those mundanes who freaked out when they saw a supernatural, although crazy robots trumped shifters in my book.

The creak of more robots made me wonder if I'd misjudged this plan. The woman screamed.

"There's a kitty in the pool!"

Good, she was funnelling them to me, using the distraction. The swoosh of electric doors told me she'd made it outside. I pounced, barrelling the first robot over and into another. The second fell and took out a third like a robot domino. As it righted itself, I leapt, extending my claws and ripping into the wires that connected its head to its body. The machine stilled, lifeless.

Something gripped my tail, and I whirled, gnashing my teeth. I let out a roar and ripped myself free before going for its throat. The tang of electricity stung my tongue, and I shook my head to get rid of the feeling that I'd licked a battery. I needed to get out of here.

The door opened. I took my chance, leaping over the assembled robots in a single bound. At the front desk, I shifted back.

"I need my bag, please."

"Valuables are returned on exit."

"I'm exiting. Now."

"You are not relaxed." The creepy not human receptionist smiled at me and I lost my cool. Robot piece of schiztz. I vaulted over the desk, shoving the receptionist bot to the floor. I took the key card from around my neck and jammed it into the small slot marked with a lock. My bag appeared on the conveyor belt, and I snagged it, feeling inside for my loaded crossbow.

Two robots whirred behind me, arms outstretched. I clicked off the safety, aimed and there was one less robot in this place. The second rammed into the desk, unable to climb over it. I scoffed.

"You need to relax. All humans must relax," creepy receptionist piped up from the floor, that stupid grin still on her fake face. I stomped my foot through the robot on the floor. The robot on the other side shuddered to a halt. There, I'd taken out the lead robot. No more AI. I sauntered over to collect my clothes when I heard a beeping sound that made the hairs on the back of my neck stand on end. The robot rebooted.

"Miss Jones, we are the SpAI and you must relax."

I rooted around in my enchanted bag and grabbed my phone. Time to call for back-up. I stared at the screen. No signal. Out of the corner of my eye I caught the no phones sign on the desk. Dzrak it.

More of the dzraking robots wheeled into the reception area, blocking my exit and fixing their electric blue eyes on me. Right. I needed to take out the heart of this spa – the AI itself. If any of the rest of the team were here, they would come up with a sophisticated plan. Maybe they'd try to reprogramme the software or something. All I knew was that no technology could function without its power source.

I held up my hands. "OK, you got me. I'll do as you ask. But first, I have a question…"

"I can answer anything in any style you choose thanks to advanced chat AI." Twelve pairs of robot eyes blinked at me as they responded in unison.

I grabbed the jug of mineral water from the desk and held it up like I was about to pour myself a glass. "Where is the power source for this place?" I paused. "Answer me like the King of England."

"Electricity cables lead to the basement."

"Fascinating. And where is the basement?"

"You can reach the basement through the door at the end of the left-hand corridor, but it is out of bounds for our spa guests. The treatment rooms are this way."

"Thanks, suckers."

I shifted into my lynx form and bolted for the basement door. I sprinted, not slowing, as I crashed through the door and down the stairs, the robots screeching behind me. The whirr of fans almost deafened me as I dived between towering grey servers with blinking lights. The AI. A voice came over the speaker system.

"Guests are not allowed in the server room. Animals are not permitted in the spa."

I shifted back to my human form, the jug of water materialising with me. I chucked it at the servers and smiled as electricity fizzed before the machine powered down with a whine and a smell of burning.

"Guests are not allowed in the server room." The clunk of feet descending metal stairs reverberated through the room. Dzraking androids. I slammed my fist into a couple of other servers for good measure, the pain spiking my adrenaline. The footsteps kept coming.

I spun to see the receptionist android reaching for me, a blank look on its symmetrical face. I ducked and kicked out. The robot jumped over my leg with lightning-fast reflexes. What the dzrak had they programmed it to do? I stood and aimed a flurry of punches at its dented stomach area. It backed up and blocked, matching my speed. I panted. This wasn't getting me anywhere.

The shift rippled through my body, and I charged it in my lynx form. It sidestepped. I used the servers as a springboard and leapt through the air, raking down with my sharp claws, taking a chunk out of its head and ruining the symmetry. It stayed standing.

I ran at it again. As it stepped to the side, I shifted back to my human form, changing attack and gripping its arms. I spun, building momentum, and launched it at one of the server stacks. It fell to the ground, twitching and smoking.

I snorted at the electrical fumes and walked out of the basement as the flames took hold. The other robots were silent sentinels as I moved past. Disconnected from the servers, they were useless. I prodded one in the chest as I passed, to make sure. No response. I grinned and went to get my clothes.

I exited the dressing room to find the fire had taken hold, flames already licking the reception desk. I didn't stop to wonder about the lack of fire alarm or sprinklers. Instead, my smile broadened.

"Now, I'm relaxed."

I stumbled outside, heat from the flames licking at my skin as I sank to the pavement. The old lady stood next to a taxi.

"Thank you."

"No problem." I waved off her gratitude.

"Do you need a ride?"

I shook my head.

"Well, if you ever need anything, you give me a call." She handed me a business card, and I stared at it. What sort of old lady carried a business card? The shiny letters proclaimed her as Elaine Merchant. Whoever that was. I put it into my handbag and opened my mouth to thank her, but the taxi had already pulled away.

I called in the fire and took a swig of the emergency water I always carried in my bag. A horn blared. I looked up to see the Magical Liaison Office van veer into the carpark before screeching to a halt. The team got out and stared at me.

Dot removed the sparkling party hat from her head. "How was the spa day?"

"Good. I rescued an old lady and defeated an evil AI. Standard day at the office."

Maxi's jaw hung open as he took in the burning building. "What? How?"

I stood and patted him on the back. "I'll tell you all about it at The Goat. I need a drink."

I climbed into the van, letting Aloora drive us the short distance to our favourite drinking hole. I'd had enough of machines for one day. Instinctively, I checked my phone. Fifty alerts flashed at me. Medusa…statues…naked wizard…the alerts went on.

"What's all this about?" I waved my screen at the team, noticing the way Maxi winced as he strapped himself in and the rip in Dot's chunky cardigan.

Dot flashed me a grin that showed her pointed teeth. "Tell you about it over drinks."

If you enjoyed reading these stories, please leave a review on amazon, goodreads or bookbub. And you can read a bonus short story about how Agent Jones and Maxi first met:

https://books.gemmaclatworthy.com/hellhound-of-the-baskervilles

Did you spot any typos? Let me know by dropping me an email at gemma@gemmaclatworthy.com

A Note from the Author

The Swindon magic roundabout is a real feature in the town. I can neither confirm nor deny if there are demons underneath it, but it is a nightmare to drive around.

The elven town and reserve of Breconia are both fictional, although there is a real town in Wales called Brecon which I'd encourage you to visit. There are also some lovely walks nearby, but watch out for rogue manticores!

There are no AI spas that I am aware of in Cardiff, but if a robot tells you to relax, run the other way!

Thank you

A special thank you to my amazing patrons: Emma Ward, Mark Canty and Bevan Clatworthy who always support me.

If you want to support Gemma, you can find her on www.patreon.com/G_Clatworthy for exclusive first reads of new stories.

You can also join her newsletter for at www.gemmaclatworthy.com for a free prequel to her Rise of Dragons series and a free short story based on one of the Omensford witches. You can follow Gemma on www.instagram.com/gemmaclatworthy, www.facebook.com/gemmaclatworthy or join the Facebook reader's group Gemma's book wyrms.

Other Books by G Clatworthy

Books in the Rise of the Dragons series:

Awakening

Solstice of Dragons

Equinox Betrayal

Darkest Deception

Attack on Avalon

Fated Bloodlines

Eat, Pray, Dragons

Books in the Omensford series (set in the Rise of the Dragons universe):

Bedsocks and Broomsticks

Cream Teas and Crystal Balls

Donkeys and Demons

Pumpkins and Popstars

Exes and Enchantments

Fae and Familiars

Gnomes and Necromancy

Books in the Saffron Vale series (a cozy fantasy series, part of the Cozy Vales universe):

A Colour to Dye For

Going for Guild

Commission Impossible

Short stories based on board games:

Ghostel

Haunticulture

Children's Books

The Child Who series:

The Girl Who Lost Her Listening Ears

The Boy Who Lost His Listening Ears

The Girl Who Dreamed of Sleep

The Boy Who Dreamed of Sleep

Nanny Pastry series:

Nanny Pastry and the Nimble Ninjabread Man

Other books:

Coronavirus in the words of children

About the Author

Gemma started writing during the 2020 lockdown and loves fantasy fiction and dragons in particular. She lives in Wiltshire with her family and two cats and also enjoys crafts of all kinds. You can see all her writing on www.patreon.com/G_Clatworthy. Join the conversation at Gemma's book wyrms readers' group on Facebook.

She also writes children's books. You can find out more on her website www.gemmaclatworthy.com or follow her on Instagram (www.instagram.com/gemmaclatworthy) or Facebook (www.facebook.com/gemmaclatworthy).